# Galactic Mandate

## A Radical Cause

By M.R. Richardson

## Acknowledgement

I like to thank my beautiful girlfriend Jodi for being the only beta reader. Her input during this process was essential to making my dream become a reality. Thank you to everyone I have met along the way who have given me advice and so much useful information. I could not have done this without the support of my convention friends, professional authors, close friends, and family.

# Table of Contents

# *Prologue*

A clear, simulated sky covered the dome, its fake sun feeling just as warm as any real one. Insects buzzed around, birds chirped, and the tropical bio-dome was full of life. Devante, a timid boy, sat near his father, Reign, waiting for the hover car to arrive. It wasn't long before an immense tank-like vehicle pulled up, loaded with all the hunting gear they required.

"Take this shotgun," Reign ordered. Looking down, he saw Devante's eyes raised with concern. "It will get the job done quickly. Trust me. You don't want this to linger on."

Devante stopped inspecting the gun and jumped aboard the hovering SUV. Then they were off on their journey to complete the hunt.

About forty-five minutes passed while they tracked broken branches, searching for their prey. Frustrated at not finding anything, the driver called out, "We can always call it a day. There'll be plenty of hunting to do tomorrow."

"Hell no," yelled Reign. "I paid good money for this. We get this done or we stay out here."

Devante felt his sense of relief fade away at his father's words. Suddenly, a bush shook, and the driver fired at it. Laser fire scorched the air as he took two quick shots.

The entire party set out on foot, rushing after their quarry. Devante quickly outpaced his father, following close behind the driver, who was an expert tracker. Soon, they heard a human voice up ahead shouting, "Ahh!" This was followed by a thud. Suddenly, a rock struck the driver's face, and he smacked against the ground with another thud.

Devante looked down, his eyes focused on the sight before him. His mouth curled down in a frown, and his eyes watered. The emotions flooding through him made his skin crawl with horror. An exact copy of himself stared back, equally shocked.

The firm hands of his father came to rest on his shoulders. "Take the shot, son."

# Chapter 1

The Galactic Planetary League had called its members to recognize Tyron Jamal of the Acolytes. As a principal member of the galactic security council, with veto rights, the elderly President Sky Lova Chatavic, his hair white and his clothes as ornate as the room, introduced Tyron to the members who had gathered to hear his speech.

Tyron surveyed the room to see who was there. The room was full of colorful, traditional outfits from each planet. The members of the Clone Defense Force sat opposite him, their delegation the only one as large as his. They stood out because of their triplet clone assistants—they seemed to organize their clones in threes in formal settings. The air was pleasant and perfumed. The climate was routinely rotated, and today's was a forest, giving the room a woody smell. Tyron's tongue could still taste the sweet fruits of the cafeteria. It was a departure from the fancy restaurants he was accustomed to, but there was no time to dwell on that today.

"The Acolyte Empire," he said to the group, "under the guidance of our ruler, the living God, has vetoed the ban of nuclear and conventional weapons. What should be banned are the laser weapons that the CDF peddles. They are just trying to sell overpriced weapons to planets and governments that are foolish enough to buy them. Most of the independent planets would be forced to modernize, which is obviously a ploy."

The dignitaries of the independent planets, who sat in the middle of the room, mostly nodded in agreement. Mycelia, the head ambassador for the CDF, stood in defiance. Her clones immediately sat down and looked at the floor. "Nonsense," she said. "Ever since Tyron got his anti-cloning legislation on the docket, he's been trying to push more and more of this anti-CDF agenda." The others looked at Tyron with a cynical eye.

"The Acolytes want to disarm us so we can't resist their aggression," stated Ambassador Deshaun Young. "There have been roaming fleets out destroying worlds. And no one knows who is doing it. How will we protect ourselves against pirates and thieves? I don't know about you, but on my planet, Donwait, we don't have defense platforms and huge armadas. We need everything we can get," he finished, to much applause from the room.

The loud bang of a mallet on a reinforced desk pierced through the noise. "Settle down. I will not have conspiracy theories enter these chambers," said Sky.

"You are on the Acolyte's dime. You are corrupt," said Jan Lee, a young minister from Planet Kubai.

"How dare you? I should bar your entire delegation," Sky replied, and the room erupted in a sudden argument.

"Don't get caught between a rock and a hard place!" Deshaun shouted.

"The CDF is nothing but slavers, and they deserve everything they get," said Rasheed, one of the Acolytes' closest allies.

"They'll conquer all of you. The imperialists never stop. God-Reign is a false god!" Mycelia shouted.

The various cronies of each faction started to actually fight, lifting their seats and physically hurling them at each other, running over to delegates from opposing countries and punching them in the face. Tyron was hurried out by his Imperial Guard, as his underlings rushed in to join the sudden brawl that had unfolded. Sky and Mycelia were also escorted out from separate exits.

Once in the hall, Tyron smiled. His job was never done—it was never considered a success. *Anytime the Galactic Congress is derailed, it's technically a success, but how will my many different masters perceive this?* Tyron thought while rushing to his assigned room. When they were safely down the hall, he and his guards realized the immediate danger was gone. *Now to report to my superiors*, he thought as he reached the door.

In her room, Mycelia poured herself a pink alcoholic concoction. It smelled only of dragon fruit, but it was special. It was infused with forbidden mutations of various kinds. They had a very potent and intoxicating effect. Drinking too much would impair the drinker's judgment and then deliver an unprecedented high. The drink was highly addictive, and this was her third glass this evening.

"What is this I hear?" asked Teresa, the foreign affairs minister. "Are you promising more protection contracts for the independent planets? We can't afford to do more than what we are doing. Cancel this deal right now."

"They are scared. They don't know what will happen," Mycelia replied.

"You know as well as I do that we can't afford to extend protection to any new planets. We are overstretched and plagued with defections. You need to face the new reality. We are not in the position we used to be fifty years ago. The legacy of the genetic war bankrupted us. Cancel the contracts, or I will replace you with someone who will." Teresa discontinued the connection.

Mycelia's lone assistant had various forms ready on data pads that demanded Mycelia's immediate attention. She gave them her signature and unique ID. "All right, out!" she commanded.

The assistant left the door open while the representatives from the united independent planets came strolling in. Their faces were covered with fresh scrapes, minor cuts, and bruises from the earlier altercation. "You have some news for us? Did your chancellor approve the deal?"

Frustrated, Mycelia poured another pink drink. "Unfortunately, I have some bad news."

# Chapter 2

The white ships moved steadily towards their target. Automated drones identified them but ignored their presence. Alarms flared, and workers bustled about on the defense platform. Commander Agrippa looked down at his viewscreen, which usually presented nothing but a boring glimpse of space.

"Command, we have a problem."

"What is it?" the command center replied.

"Unknown ships have been detected, but our scanners can't lock onto them."

"Defend this capital. If anything happens to the homeworld, it will be your court-martial." The transmission ended.

Agrippa gripped the railing, observing the command center of the defense platform. "Hail those ships. Give them ten seconds to respond and then blast them out of the sky."

"How are we going to destroy the ships?" asked Castor, a young ensign. He'd just started his first rotation on the planetary defense platform, and he was clearly overwhelmed. "We can't get a lock with any of the weapons."

"Fire blindly if you have to. Alert all the other platforms that we will have to give them everything."

"Ten … nine … eight … seven … six … five…" Castor began, and then he interrupted the countdown to deliver the message: "All the other platforms are out of range. Looks like it's just us, sir."

Agrippa nodded, and Castor continued: "Four … three … two…"

The ships started to respond. A strange clicking sound played over the platform's stereo.

The room was plunged into darkness for the faintest couple of seconds. Then emergency lighting filled the void, generating a harsh, shadowy atmosphere that matched the situation. "We lost power to the main cannons. We won't be able to fire," Castor stated.

A burst of light seared through the dimly lit room as an explosion deafened the crew. Agrippa abandoned his post, racing with crewmates to find a spacesuit. There weren't many available, but the repeated bombardment made sure there were fewer and fewer people to compete for the ones left. Agrippa grabbed a headpiece and some gloves. He didn't bother with the rest. After stopping to help a few of his subordinates find and attach their gear, he went back towards the panel opposite the guide lights.

He found his command chair and then rebooted the viewports. The monitor showed that the white fleet had left, but a long, cylindrical white ship was cruising past the platform. Dozens of black spots began to appear. *Missile launcher*, he thought. Slowly, warheads marked with a nuclear symbol began to emerge.

Agrippa primed the launch system and loaded in the codes to get the platform ready to fire. He was as excited as a little boy, his palms sweaty inside his gloves, when red targeting circles lit up on his monitor. He squeezed with no hesitation, firing on the cylindrical ship.

Too late. He watched the missiles from the other ship trace their way to the imperial capital of Emortono. His eyes trembled when he saw the mushroom clouds rise from the planet below. Mixed emotions flowed through him as the enemy ship broke apart while, behind it, the planet glowed from the nuclear blasts.

# Chapter 3

Devante watched the news broadcast of the trial of Agrippa Sagot. Images of the devastated imperial capital were replayed with a warning of their graphic nature. Only the leaders of a few minor factions were there. Most of the great imperial leaders had stayed in their fiefdoms. The loss of the capital had not created a leadership void, but the bureaucracy was a pain in the ass. The loss of life numbered in the millions. Turning the monitor off, Devante's eyes teared up. "That's enough of that."

"This tragedy still hurts me as much as the first day I heard it, sir," a councilman offered.

"We all have lost family, pride, and so much more," Devante replied.

"It's only been three days. We all need time to process this, to contact family and loved ones," said Commander Kai. He was sitting in the corner of the room, looking at pictures of family members who would never contact him again.

Devante stood up, puffing out his chest while letting the tears recede from his eyes. Quickly, he glared at the empty seat of his greatest commander. The others followed his eyes, but they quickly returned their focus to Devante again. "This is obviously an attempt to punish me personally. To break my resolve. The CDF won't be allowed to continue these attacks on our civilians, our family, our children—"

"But we don't know if it is the CDF," said Kai. "The ships were unmarked, and they did not show any trace of the clone's forces."

"That changes nothing!" exclaimed Devante. "The timing suggests this is an attempt to punish us because of our resolution in the Galactic Planetary League to ban cloning. This won't stop my resolve. This won't stop me from getting justice for our fallen compatriots, our fallen citizens."

Commander Kai's face was red, his eyes filled with passion. "That won't bring my family back. My wife and my two beautiful daughters. They were taken away from me by those bastards."

Another commander in the opposite corner looked up and said, "What about our families who are still living? How do we keep them safe?"

The chirping of an incoming transmission stopped the conversation. Five large monitors lit up in a widescreen view of Emperor God-Reign. "We keep them safe with peace. Peace is the only answer for limiting needless violence, which we have already seen. I order you all to de-escalate this meeting at once. There shall be no more talk of revenge and how you will strike this or strike that. The Intelligence Bureau has been analyzing the wreckage but has not come up with anything. Devante, as my firstborn and heir, I want you to lead the investigation. We will root out who did this to us, and we will negotiate peace." The transmission ended swiftly.

Devante gritted his teeth. Feigning a smile, he turned to the room and said, "Justice will be served. Do not worry." He looked at the seat of his missing fleet commander and smiled.

# Chapter 4

His tongue swirled, enthralling his mistress. The chancellor moaned, telling him to go faster or slower. The muscular hunk grabbed her hips with a firm but gentle grip. She appreciated the delicate care he took with pleasing her. She looked down to make eye contact, but her gaze drifted to his tattoos, lingering on the "XXL5496" that ran across his face in bold, horizontal letters. His two duplicates waited with their backs against the wall, their heads down. The only difference between them was the last digit of their tattoos. A beep interrupted her pleasure.

"Chancellor. You are needed on the bridge," one of the crewmen said.

"Unmute... I'll be there shortly," she replied as her clone stopped his licking.

The duplicates of XXL5496 quickly grabbed some clothing for the chancellor to wear. They seemed relieved as she got dressed. She knew they were going to the private gym in her quarters. Although they were naturally muscular, they enjoyed working out to maintain their physiques.

*** 

Hovering above Planet VFA-T10, the chancellor's flagship monitored the communications and tactical positions of the local inhabitants. The chancellor entered the bridge, eyeing the ship's name displayed overhead: *Freedom Fall*. It was a newer ship but made to be disposable. She remembered the days when the Clone Defense Force could have afforded dozens of these. The recession, brought on by investor nervousness due to the recent resolutions in the Galactic Planetary League, had changed all that. It was truly remarkable how coffers of credits could disappear. Not that she cared about money, but you couldn't defend a republic on a tight budget.

"Glad you are on the bridge, Chancellor."

"What's the situation, Lieutenant Anderson?"

"Things are changing fast on the ground. The sultan of this third-world planet supports us, but he has lost the support of his governors. His castle is currently under siege by rebels. Should we bomb them and prop up our ally?"

"No. The tide has changed. Let's change with it."

"Are you sure? Sultan Trajan has been one of our oldest allies. He supported us in this hostile region when no one else would."

"Unless you want to lose your job, I suggest you give the rebels air support," the chancellor commanded.

Lieutenant Anderson turned to his corporals. Their clean, matching gray uniforms reminded him of the white uniforms the clone soldiers wore. "Launch the fighters and two squadrons of bombers," he ordered. "Level the sultan's castle and destroy all military targets. You have twenty-four hours to complete this task."

"Yes, Lieutenant. The clones will get this done," one of the corporals replied.

The viewscreen displayed the departure of the clone fighters.

"The Congress has requested a meeting," Lieutenant Anderson informed the chancellor. "They want to go over our plans for the Acolytes."

"I bet they do, Lieutenant. We won't allow the Acolytes to disrupt our cloning any longer. The Clone Defense Force will not be at the mercy of religious zealots. If you perform well, Anderson, I might even get you and your wife some clones to celebrate our victory."

Lieutenant Anderson grinned. He seemed to be thinking of all the money that would be saved if he got a pack of clones as a gift.

The chancellor entered the conference room. Holograms of important ministers sat across from each other, and representative of her political party and opposition parties sat staring at the monitors in the room.

"Why haven't we declared open war on the Acolytes yet?" her party's chairmen asked. The room broke out in a mild murmur of agreement.

"Gentlemen, this is why none of you will ever be elected chancellor. You lack the finesse that is needed. I'm glad I'm grooming future leaders who can handle these kinds of problems if anything were to happen to me. We don't need and cannot afford a war with the Acolytes. That's why we shall continue our clandestine campaign." She took a deep breath, giving herself time to read the room, looking for signs of unsettled men and women. "I have plans for the Acolytes. Let me get everyone up to speed."

***

XXXL5496, or Ninety-six, as he liked to think of himself, lifted the bar from his chest, his arms aching. He had to do a little more than the others to keep his status as favorite. *I want freedom*, he thought, weights clanking around him. *Just being some woman's toy, this isn't enough for me. What is out there? What planet are we even hovering above? What kind of entertainment do the natties get into?*

"Do you ever wonder what's out there?" Ninety-eight asked.

*It's like he read my mind.* Ninety-six had never gotten used to the synergy that he and his clone brothers had. He preferred the company of natties; it was just less creepy. "I was thinking about that, actually. But you don't want to know what happened to Ninety-seven. He thought about leaving, and he tried to overpower Judy. Can you guess what happened next?"

"She activated his implants?" Ninety-eight guessed while Ninety-nine looked on.

"Worse. Judy never got to it. She didn't need to. Turns out they monitor her body. Yeah, the pervs, right? Well, a team came in here and threw him out the airlock faster than I could blink. She killed Ninety-five to make sure I wouldn't try it either."

"Damn, that's horrible," said Ninety-eight. "No trial or jury?"

Ninety-six laughed, putting a hand up to stop the others from talking. "A trial?" He laughed again as he went back to working out.

"You should try. It's better than living in this room for the rest of your life. I bet Ninety-nine doesn't even know what the rest of the ship looks like," Ninety-eight stated.

"I do too."

"No, you don't!" Ninety-six yelled.

"If anyone's going to get away with it, it'd be her favorite," Ninety-nine said.

Ninety-six started to think he was right. "Maybe I should give it a try."

# *Chapter 5*

"Commander Kai, I have a mission for you."

Kai turned and faced his leader with anticipation.

"It's black ops," continued Devante, "so you will be on your own this time. Do you think you can handle that?"

"Of course. Whatever I can do to keep this empire safe and get it back to normal is fine with me."

"Great. I need you to take the *DKR* and investigate Dr. Ulises Toms on Planet Mockzima. Be careful. The machine men are not to be trifled with."

Kai's eyes opened wide. "The *DKR* is a joke. It's an old, bloated battlecruiser that's one hit away from becoming space junk."

"Didn't you just say you'd do anything to keep the empire safe?"

"Yes, but that doesn't mean I don't need the proper tools. There must be a better ship."

"Anything newer and the machine men will disable it like they did our homeworld's platforms. I'm going to need someone who is willing to do whatever it takes on this one. I need someone who can think creatively. Someone willing to do more than just say some words to keep this empire safe. Is that you?"

Kai stood and saluted. "Sir, yes, sir."

"Remember, the doctor's capture and interrogation are vital to our security. Off you go." Devante headed past Kai and down the halls to his garden, one of the finest around.

Kai turned and walked to the shuttle bay. He needed to ship out. His time on the luxury cruiser Devante commanded was over.

***

Eight hours later, Kai arrived at the rustic *DKR*, a battlecruiser from a bygone era. While approaching the ship, he noticed the repair crew sparking and sizzling new welds on the ship's exterior...iron and dirty, rusty-looking pipes flowed across the exterior of the ship. If the ship were to fall apart in front of his eyes, he wouldn't be surprised.

The shuttle door opened, and he was greeted by two of the *DKR*'s command team: the big and tall Lieutenant Micah Emil and, to his right, the Shock General Lasondra Washington, a muscular woman for whom battle readiness was a religion.

More sparks and more repairs went on in the background. How this ship would ever fly, much less stay in space, was beyond Kai. "Set a course for Mockzima. We leave in twenty-four hours."

"I'll tell the troops to write their last wills and testaments, and I'll ready some caskets. That planet is a death sentence," Lasondra proclaimed.

Kai didn't bother to put up a front. She was right. This journey would mean plenty of deaths for her troops. "Let's just hope it's a limited engagement. He mostly keeps to himself."

"Any news from Intelligence? Do they know who struck us yet?" Micah asked.

"That's what we are going to find out. Prince Devante knows that the only people who could bypass our targeting systems the way they did would be the machine men. So, we are gambling on one of their scientists to get to the bottom of it."

The soldiers shrugged and then left, leaving Kai with his shuttle captain, who happily showed the commander to his quarters. *Once I get some sleep, the adventure begins*, Kai thought.

***

As the dropship plunged toward the planet's surface, Commander Kai observed his squad of black ops marines.

Then he looked out the windows at the planet outside. It was mostly barren and uninhabitable, with lots of volcanic rock. Bare deserts of dry, boring scenery whizzed by. The marines were silent, like a funeral was coming. It seemed appropriate that everyone was dressed in black. Kai turned to Lasondra. Her face was pointed to the windows, deep in thought. Yesterday, when he had met her, she had been filled with angst, anticipating a fight. That emotion had seemingly turned into dread at the thought of their opponent.

"All right, I'll have to drop you off in the forest around the lab," said Emil. "Don't want to get hit by air defense. They are already buzzing my sensors now."

They set down in a forest, and everyone scurried out of the dropship. The forest was sparsely populated with trees. Kai watched as a rookie tried to rest his hands on one, only to fall through it. "A hologram?" the rookie asked from the ground.

Lasondra turned back and said, "They all are. There is no life in this forest."

"Except us," Kai replied. He looked around and finally noticed that all the trees were exactly the same. Lasondra was right. They were all holograms. *Lazy*, he thought.

It took about fifteen minutes to slowly make their way to the gigantic laboratory, which was one large tower. It sat on a large piece of land in the middle of an island with cliffs on all sides. A bridge connected the island to the mainland, and it was a long way down to the water and rocks below.

Kai and his black ops team approached the bridge. As commander, he had to make the first step onto the bridge. His squad closely watched him to make sure it was safe. The bridge was made up of hands from the machine men, who had formed their own, larger tower at the midpoint of the bridge. They were also stationed at both ends of the bridge.

As Kai and his squad traversed the bridge, the silver machine men would climb across the bodies of their fellows to form the missing steps of the bridge, Once the group had passed, with clanking bodies, the machine men would disassemble the previously made bridge. When the group was safely across, two larger guards slid heavy metal doors into their sockets to let Kai and his squad into the lab.

Inside, Kai and his squad moved from room to room, looking for Dr. Tom. They followed the sounds of mechanical laughter until, finally, they reached the main lab. It was a large room with all types of electronics scattered about. Hovering experiments and monitors lined the walls. A large viewscreen that took up one wall cycled through equations, occasionally stopping for input.

"Doctor Tom," said Kai.

"Yes." A machine man moved forward. Two others guarded him on his left and right.

"You are under arrest for crimes against the Acolyte Empire." Kai's squad moved up, firing electromagnetic restraints that captured the doctor and his two henchmen.

"Ugh. What is this about?" Dr. Tom asked.

"The Emortono attack on us. We believe you had something to do with the tech used," Kai replied.

"Of course I did," said Dr. Tom. "I have the best technology, and you bumbling meat bags will never match it."

Kai examined the doctor. He was different from the machine men outside. Though his legs and arms were the same wireframe metal, the core of his body was organic. His head was a metal wire frame over human eyes, a brain encased in a metal skull, and what looked to be a human mouth and throat. "So, you admit it? You don't even deny it?" Kai asked, shocked at such bluntness.

"I'm playing a game much bigger than you or even your empire can imagine. My research into the ancients won't be stopped. Progress cannot be stopped!" Dr. Tom shouted.

Kai laughed. "Researching the ancients. That doesn't sound like progress to me. Sounds like you don't even know which way is up anymore. All these doctorates on your wall were wasted on nothing but a mechanical terrorist."

The room went dark, and then red lights flashed on. An alarm blared in the background. Kai heard the clanking of metal above, and he looked up to see machine men crawling across the ceiling toward them, their red eyes staring at him and his squad.

Lasondra screamed into the communicator on her wrist for reinforcements as the fight started. Blaster fire filled the air, and machine men started dropping to the ground. Kai watched as the rookie of the group shot up, directly above himself. "Don't do that!" he yelled, but it was too late. A lifeless machine body fell and crushed the rookie.

Kai and Lasondra's troops moved with military precision to the exit, hauling their prisoners in tow. Blaster fire continued to rage as they ran down the hallways. Machine men smashed their fists through the walls, crushing the heads of unsuspecting marines with their metal hands. Soon, the only marines left were those holding the prisoners captive.

"I've got an idea!" Lasondra yelled. She overcharged her blaster and aimed it directly at a wall, blasting a large hole to the outside. "Follow me," she ordered as the rest of the men and hostages filed through.

Once outside, they heard the thundering sound of hundreds of machine men crawling towards them. The tower at the middle of the bridge grew larger and fuller as machine men crawled to join it. Dozens of mechanical arms reached out. Kai was distracted from this by the screams of two of his black ops marines as they were dragged over the edge of the cliff. Lasondra smacked her used-up blaster against the fingers of machine men as they tried to crawl up and over the edge of the cliff. The leaning tower of machine men grabbed the remaining marines, throwing them all over the edge. Then it grabbed the captive machine men, slowly lowering them down the tower until they were out of sight.

The tower swung back, preparing to grab Kai, Lasondra, and Dr. Tom. Just then, dropships appeared over their position. A powerful laser blast cut through the tower, sending half of it into an uncontrolled fall into the lab. Lasondra, Dr. Tom, and Kai had to run to avoid the rain of metal bodies that came crashing down around them. Dr. Tom used the opportunity to push off the wall and roll off the cliff. Machine hands grabbed onto him, slowing his fall, as he snowballed down the side.

"Don't worry, Commander. The cavalry has come," a static-filled voice said in Kai's ear. Suddenly, towers of machine men, even larger than before, reached up and grabbed the dropships, pulling them down to the ground and causing some to explode.

As the battle raged around them, Kai touched the communicator on his wrist and yelled, "Get me and Lasondra out of here!"

"What about the rest of your team?" Emil asked.

"They didn't make it, and neither will we if you don't hurry."

A dropship started firing rapidly and in different directions, laying down cover for its quick path to Kai and Lasondra. Groups of machine men formed towers to stop the dropship, but a couple of ships slammed into them at high speeds, smashing them into debris. Lasondra and Kai lay down fire, desperately trying to kill the enemy. The dropship finally reached their position, and it hovered in front of them as the door swung open. "Lieutenant?" Kai asked.

"Get in!" Emil yelled.

Kai jumped in, and then he looked back at Lasondra. Before she could jump into the dropship, machine men grabbed her legs, arms, and head. Blaster fire erupted all around as her black ops marines jumped out of the dropship to help.

At the bottom of the cliffs, arrow-shaped ships emerged and rocketed into the sky. As the dropship door closed, Kai looked out the window and saw another arrow ship slam into the cliffside that Lasondra and her loyal troopers were making their last stand on. The explosion turned everything on the cliffside into paste.

"No! Lasondra!" Kai screamed.

"She's gone, Commander." Emil grabbed Kai's shoulder in a firm, comforting grasp. "Commence aerial bombardment," he ordered over the radio as they flew back to the *DKR*. Missiles streaked through the sky as they flew past, erupting in flashes of light behind them.

"The situation has changed. Dr. Tom has gotten away," Kai said.

"Not yet," Emil replied.

The voice of a communications officer came over the radio. "*DKR* to Commander Kai, we are taking some serious damage up here."

"How so?" Kai asked.

"The machine men are flying kamikaze into the ship, sir."

"Looks like several are trying to get away as well." Emil pointed to one of the ship's monitors, and Kai noticed a small group veering off from the attack and forming around a central ship. "That's him, He's trying to escape." To the communications officer, he said, "*DKR*, scramble all fighters to protect while we pursue the target."

Emil piloted the ship away from their current course toward the *DKR* and instead went to follow the strays. Soon, they were in weapons range. Assuming the protected ship in the center of the four escorts was the doctor's, they engaged. Their laser blasted, and one of the escorts exploded, leaving three more. Two of the enemy ships broke off and turned towards Kai's dropship. Kai got in a gunner's seat and fired desperately. The machine men fighters turned and spun away, dodging the dropship's laser as they came near. They did not have offensive weapons, but if they crashed into the dropship, they would explode like a giant ordinance.

Wild blasts seared past the fighters as Kai pulled the trigger quickly and without discretion. Finally, his lasers met one of the ships, destroying it. The debris spun into the other, destroying it as well so that the path to the final two ships was clear.

Suddenly, there was a boom and a bam. "I couldn't get clear of those destroyed ships quick enough. That debris really got us," said Emil's co-pilot, Philandro.

"Looks like one of the ships is sending a transmission," Emil said.

Kai looked at the information panels, taking a second to catch a deep breath and calm himself down. All the adrenaline from the chase had made him a bit jittery. Quickly, he turned on the transmission-tapping counter-surveillance system.

Dr. Tom's voice came on the dropship's speaker system. "I need an extraction; the Acolytes are on my tail."

"We won't pick you up unless you have what we agreed on."

"I do, I do. Come quickly. I won't last long out here."

"Not unless you have what we agreed upon."

"I have the targets and the program to disable them. Pick me up, or they die with me," Dr. Tom stated.

Kai yelled out, "We got him! I'm targeting the ship that sent that transmission." He moved his targets to the machine man ship and pulled the trigger. Unfortunately, the last remaining escort ship spun in front of the shot, taking the full blast. It exploded.

"I won't be able to avoid this wreck," said Philandro.

Boom!!!

"We've stopped."

"Pursue him," Kai ordered.

"We can't," Lieutenant Emil replied.

"We are drifting while that fucking terrorist plots to kill innocent people."

"The *DKR* is en route to pick us up."

The proximity alarm blared as the white fleet appeared from zero space.

"Order the *DKR* to engage. Fire everything we've got at it," Kai ordered.

"Yes, sir," Emil replied, and then he relayed the orders to the approaching battlecruiser.

*The white fleet looks just as it did when it attacked my homeworld*, Kai thought. He realized that he had an opportunity to end it all quickly. He took his wrist communicator and called Fleet Command. "We have the unknown fleet in our sights. Send us reinforcements, and we can take them down. Relay this to Dark Reign."

"Yes, sir. I have a couple of ships in the area I can send before I get authorization from Dark Reign to send the main fleet. You will need to hold out for a couple of hours. Fleet Command out."

"A few hours? Get here NOW!!!" Kai yelled. But there was no answer. The line had already disconnected.

The dropship watched as the unknown fleet's main battleship opened its docking bay, letting the doctor's ship in. The *DKR*'s barrage of fire started in the background.

"We can slow them down if we ram the *DKR* into their ships," said Kai. "If we plan the course correctly, it could disable half of the fleet."

"Are you crazy? That would kill everyone on board!" Emil exclaimed.

"We must do whatever it takes," Kai replied. "Give the..."

The white ships left into zero space, their fleet shields intact.

"Fleet Command, this is Commander Kia. Call off the reinforcements. The cowards, they ran."

"Mantis is going to secure your ship and lead reinforcements to your position," came the reply.

"We don't need them."

"You don't have the authority to call them off. I suggest you get your story straight by the time they arrive. Mantis is a hard-ass looking for a stepping stone to advancement, and you could be that stone. Fleet Command out."

# Chapter 6

The chancellor returned to her quarters. You could see the time on her face. "Ninety-six, get over here," she commanded in the same tone she used for her crew. She looked at herself in the mirror and snickered. "I could lose some weight.... Maybe not. A woman of my age needs to look distinguished. I'm not a sexbot like you boys."

Ninety-six continued to stir in the kitchen, eating the food his clone brother had cooked for him. He felt a shocking surge up his body: his implant. "Ninety-six, I said come here. Now, obey."

He dropped everything. He wished he could finish his meal, as the chancellor had interrupted the start of it. His stomach growled from all the working out he'd done earlier in the day.

"Sit here." The chancellor waved her hand for him to sit on the bed. She proceeded to undress, and with each article of clothing, the stress seemed to leave her body, and her face relaxed just a tad bit each time. "I was thinking about us. You know you are the clone that I have had the longest, correct?"

"Yes, it is a great honor."

"Don't you want to know about my day?" she asked as she sent a quick surge through his body.

"Yes. Sorry, I wasn't thinking. How was your day?"

"Chancellor."

"Yes, how was your day, Chancellor?"

"It was oh so tedious. I had to explain so much to those idiots on the council. They think one day they will replace me, but we all know that's not how it will go." The chancellor continued to undress until she was completely naked on the bed next to him. All of her troubles and worries had left her like her clothes, which were now spread about the room, intermixed with documents and small drives on the floor. Ninety-six's clone brothers, or duplicates, as he thought of them, sometimes took the clothing, documents, and assorted drives away. "Well, they will try, but my successor will out-politic them all through intelligence, planning, and strength of will. My daughter will become the next chancellor. There is little those morons can do to stop it."

"But your daughter will never be allowed to do that," Ninety-six replied.

"Not that one. We will make a new one."

As Ninety-six started to undress, a slight excitement overtook him. It had been a long time since he'd had sex. Impregnating the chancellor might make his position in life a little bit more enjoyable.

She stopped his rapid undressing to inform him of the rest of her plan. "Not that way, silly. She is going to be a clone, and you will carry her to term."

His eyes lit up in disbelief. "That doesn't even make sense. I don't have the right equipment. Don't you just need a lady for that?"

"Clones are so silly. I forget your education of the galaxy isn't really complete."

Still mystified, he stared at the chancellor with obvious questions in his eyes.

"The doctor will put our child in here." She touched the area below his stomach. "An artificial womb—well, they call it a hybrid male womb. You will incubate the cloned embryo until it's time for her to be born. I thought this would bring us closer. You deserve this honor. You have been loyal to me long enough. This way goes much better because a human is incubating her. But don't worry. None of your DNA will infect her with your passiveness. She will still be an exact copy of me."

His look and demeanor did not change. He sat there, still mystified, as the chancellor touched his midsection in a loving trance. His thoughts started to fly faster than the speed of light. *I'll never be able to escape if this happens. I'm done being this lady's science experiment. I'm no one's property. I don't belong to her. I didn't choose her. I want so much more for myself. How will I see the galaxy when I'm stuck raising her clone? Wait a minute. Does she want me to raise it? I bet she does. This is over. My duplicates are right. It's time.*

The chancellor motioned for his clone brothers to come over, and they all touched his stomach in anticipation of what was to come. *I'm not sure how, but I have to escape. There is no other way.*

# Chapter 7

The *Hard Prey* slipped out of zero space to approach the debris field. An open hail immediately buzzed the communications officer. On the viewport, Kai saw several salvage and repair ships launch. Quickly, they were en route to the debris field and the *DKR* itself.

"Don't worry. My salvage ships aren't going to scrap you and your command just yet," Mantis teased over the ship's monitor.

"The mission was mostly a failure. They escaped before we got on to important questions," Kai reported.

"You better get out in that field and find something useful, or I am leaving you here with your friends, the machine men. Then you can deal with this interplanetary incident you created. Who calls for reinforcements on a black ops mission anyway? I'm sure they will give you a warm welcome if you return planetside." Mantis disappeared from the monitor.

\*\*\*

Dr. Tom left his ship to meet the commanding officer, Admiral Lee. Admiral Lee stared at him with his usual look of contempt. "You really fucked up. Saving you risked the entire mission. We are here to destabilize, not save your ass all the time."

"The information I have is worth it. I just need a new untraceable ship."

"What do you think this is? A superstore?"

"Fine, whatever you have will suffice."

"Where are you going anyway? You are on one of the safest ships in the galaxy right now. Just stay here."

The clones surrounding the admiral were in special, unmarked uniforms. Each had a special attachment on his chest that Dr. Tom recognized as one of his designs. It disintegrated the wearer when life signs were no longer detected. It made evidence extremely hard to collect. Dr. Tom moved to a galactic map on the wall. One side of its display was vibrant with active ship movements. He pointed to the opposite side. "Here. I am going here. To the artifact."

Admiral Lee's eyes opened wide. "That is far across their space. Even we can't protect you there."

"I thought that wasn't your job."

"Good point."

"I'll be fine. Everyone loves Dr. Tom and what I can do for them."

"That will be a hard sell if they capture you. I don't think they need anything from us."

"They don't. Not from you."

"In three hours, you will have a suitable vessel. Your information better be good."

"The Acolytes won't know what hit them." Dr. Tom smiled.

"They better not. If it turns out to be bogus, I am coming for you, and I don't care who's space you are hiding in."

\*\*\*

Back out in a new dropship, Kai and Emil looked around the debris field, doing the boring grunt work of sorting through the wreckage for any viewable data chips.

"I think I found something!" yelled Emil. "It's an extremely damaged chip from one of the escorts we destroyed."

"That's what we need," Kai replied.

"Hopefully it's not corrupted."

"Let's get it in the analyzer."

Emil activated a tractor beam.

"Nooo," said Kai, "don't do that. It's too fragile."

"What?"

The data chip turned into dust as the tractor beam dragged it and other junk closer to the ship.

"Emil, we can't use a tractor beam on something so fragile. Did you even pass the military entrance exam?"

"Actually, no. My father was a war hero, so they were able to slide me in. I almost passed, though."

Kai's face grew flushed. "If we get out of this situation, I'm sending you for retraining."

"Sure, Commander. I'm sure Mantis or Dark Reign himself will sign off on that right now."

"He's about to sign off on sending you out the airlock," Kai blurted out. He and Emil looked at each other, then laughed.

Bang, bang, bang!

"What's that?" asked Emil as an alarm went off. A monitor displayed a metal man banging on the hull. "We are going to have to deal with that."

"Shit," Kai exclaimed. The banging continued. Kai and Emil rushed to put on spacesuits.

"Ready?" Emil asked as he rushed towards the back airlock.

"Wait," Kai ordered. "Open the back door. He's trying to get in. He'll come to us."

"Right."

The back door opened, and the machine man crawled along the spaceship's hull, clinking and clanking against it until he was almost to the rear door. The noises became silent, and then they saw a metal head slowly appear from the side of the vessel, peeking in the doorway. They fired a couple of shots and then waited. Their enemy moved back behind the corner with haste. A piece of metal flew through the open door, but it was overtaken by artificial gravity and fell to the dropship's floor. *This won't be settled without a real fight*, Kai thought.

The machine man poked his head in quickly and at different points around the door. They fired whenever they saw it, but the machine man was too fast. This frustrated everyone involved. Soon, the machine man stopped, leaving an uneasy calm. They heard him whack one of the ship's windows behind them. As they turned their heads to look, the machine man ran to the back door and then pulled and flipped himself into the ship.

He rushed at Kai and Emil, and they fired wildly, their shots hitting the walls and console but also hitting a limb. They didn't seem to slow the machine man down. He punched Kai in the chest, sending him slamming into a wall. A stray shot hit the artificial gravity console, making everyone float.

The machine man got a hold of Emil's arm, crushing it with brute force. Kai switched the projection on his laser weapon. He steadied it as the machine man's head turned to face him. He fired a wide but surgical shot that chopped the machine man's head off cleanly. He focused his weapon again and cut Emil's dead arm off, and then he watched it float off into space.

\*\*\*

"I'm glad you were able to grab the head. This is going to be very valuable," said Trayvon, the technician analyzing the severed head's memory. "So far, though, much of what we've found is nothing but boring, trivial tasks this machine completed."

"Well, there has to be something interesting, or it's my ass. You have to tell me some good news here," Kai replied.

"There is something that is odd. We keep seeing this symbol, but it doesn't make sense."

"What's that?"

"We keep seeing the Keepers symbol. It's all over these spare parts this machine man was moving around. Why would one of the Acolyte lords be working with those machine men? Especially for ship parts. Like I said, it doesn't really make sense."

"Keep this secret," Kai commanded. "I'll report this to Prince Devante only. No one else outside of this room should know about it."

A smile formed on Kai's lips.

*Finally, I got something.*

# Chapter 8

Devante's shuttle hurtled down to the seat of his family power. He was glad that the planet his family called home had been untouched in the initial attack. However, there were signs of change all around. The skyline wasn't as busy. The city was putting different fallout signs up. Shelters were now clearly labeled in case of attack. Every Wednesday, there were drills. The monitors stayed on the news, no longer playing different types of entertainment like they had a month before. Devante's shuttlecade flew to a lush mountain completely covered by green. They flew through a waterfall and into a natural valley with a mountain wall thirty stories tall. Natural and artificial waterfalls surrounded a small city. In the center of this city was a domed greenhouse larger than most but not all other city buildings. *Ah, the summer palace*, Devante thought. The sunbeam directly above the city washed the stone building with its light.

"Sir," said one of Devante's men, "we've received a high-priority communication from Commander Kai."

*Finally, some progress*, Devante thought. "Redirect the feed to my private quarters at the palace. Tell them to wait until I answer."

"Yes, sir."

The shuttle docked, and Devante walked to his room. When he was ready, he opened the channel to hear what he expected was good news. He would have the evidence he needed to bring justice to those who deserved it. He would liberate the clones and finally ban the practice over the entire galaxy. *Whoa*, Devante thought. *I'm getting ahead of myself. Time to take the first step.*

Kai's face illuminated the monitor. "I take it you have the evidence I need to get my war declaration," Devante said.

"Not exactly. We found evidence that machine men have been working with the Keepers of the Light," Kai stated.

Devante was shocked by the news. "What did you just say?"

"We were able to capture images from one of the machine men, and it clearly shows equipment from the Keepers," Kai replied.

"I put you in charge of protecting the empire. Of making sure our citizens are safe, and this is what you have for me? You accuse the biggest benefactor of my family of treason because you found some images?" Devante asked rhetorically. "Purge this information from your system. I see this was a waste of time to trust you." *This can't be. If it is true, the cause will never be able to continue.*

# Chapter 9

Jon-Kar of the planet Kublai bent to one knee, his bravery at an all-time high as he proposed to his girlfriend. Tasha Jar looked lovely as she excitedly nodded in agreement. Her face was flushed. The red sun shone brightly, giving everything a dusty, yellowish color. From the boardwalk, they could see the entire city. This was the romantic spot where they had first kissed. As she gazed into his eyes, day became night. This was startling and unsettling. It was just the afternoon; nightfall was not for hours. Tasha Jar looked up from her seated position, her eyes pointed at the sky.

First, it started as a blotch. Then it was a rectangle. Then Tasha recognized it as a ship getting closer and closer. The young couple did not yet have any reason for alarm, as they had seen many spaceships in their day. Something about this one coming toward them was captivating. The city lights automatically came on as the ship's shadow blocked out the sun. The panic started to set in as they soon recognized that this was no ordinary ship. It was a dark-green battleship coming straight at them.

The city's inhabitants started to run as the one ship became many and chaos erupted around them. Their planet had once been part of a mighty empire, but those glory days were gone now. Their limited defense force crumbled around the young couple. Fighters started falling from the sky, crashing into buildings as others exploded. The battleship that they were running from cushioned its fall using some sort of afterburners. Unmarked fighter ships flew from the sides, dark green, fully charged, and trying to cause as much damage as possible. Lifeboats shot out, flying into the ground, the buildings, and everywhere else.

The battleship tilted downward, blocking the red sun with its shadow. Then it continued moving toward the young couple on the boardwalk. The man was still on one knee, his proposal interrupted, and the woman embraced him as the battleship grew near. After a quick kiss, they watched as the ship grew bigger and bigger in the sky. Around them, people fled while they just stood there and watched. The ship looked like a giant finger pointing at them from the sky. Soon, it was so close that there was nothing else above them. The ship crashed onto the boardwalk, obliterating the couple and breaking into several pieces. Fighter jets, lifeboats, and ground assault vehicles were launched as it landed. These vehicles crashed into various parts of the city.

Kubai, the capital city of the planet with the same name, erupted into chaos. Air raid sirens blared as the battle sparked in the city.

Buildings emptied as people started fleeing in any direction they could. Personal transports flew through the air. Some were lucky enough to escape the carnage, and some were not, as they were shot down either by crossfire or intentionally by the invaders. The invaders did not show much mercy.

\*\*\*

Commander Skyfall didn't know if it was incompetence or inexperience that made the Kubai space militia retreat to the troposphere of this planet. She did not care, as she wanted victory.

On her ship hovering above the clouds, holographic displays of the active battlefield reflected off of her shining black hair. "Pull back from the surface," she commanded the special forces. Known as the angel guard, they served in God's Imperial Fleet. Right now, all insignias were missing, and there was no indication of rank or affiliation, just as she had ordered. This attack had to be officially deniable so that her ruler could not be tied or traced to it. Skyfall touched her hips as the holographic representation of her enemy's ships were shown. Instead of looking at the table display, she looked out the window. The main port showed her a better picture of what was truly happening. It was almost beautiful to see so many ships just above the clouds blasting away at each other.

"Commander?" the captain asked.

"Commander?" he repeated.

"Commander," he said finally, "the *Malevolence* has been shot down. It lies defenseless on the ground. What are your orders?"

"Leave it," she replied.

She stoked the flowers on her dress, content, as she realized she had everything she had ever wanted at this very moment.

The militia ships were concentrated in a small area. They were as dangerous as anyone backed into a corner, but on this day, their limited funds and training showed. Commander Skyfall decided that if they didn't have the proper equipment to win this battle, she would make this their literal downfall today.

"Fire the neutralizer," she commanded. The command crew looked shocked at the mention of such a devastating weapon, one they hadn't used in years.

The first blast hit, and the militia ships stopped firing back. Another blast was fired, and then the effects become obvious. Skyfall watched from the bridge's window as the militia ships started to fall to the ground, the rain of metal demolishing everything below. The capital city was destroyed, but the war was not won yet.

Two men were standing against the wall. Even without insignias, their full beards, gray hair, and perfect posture were giveaways that they were high-ranking officers.

"General Shakur," Skyfall said.

"Yes, Commander Skyfall?"

"The skies are clear. All militia ships have been neutralized. I trust you can handle the ground invasion? It should be mostly clean-up at this point."

"Yes, Commander."

"Make sure to rescue and coordinate with survivors of the *Malevolence*, if there are any."

"Right away. This planet should be under control within a week."

Skyfall walked past the officers and exited the command center bridge. She walked down the ship's halls until she reached the door to her quarters: a large room, a cabin really, comfortable and decorated with her signature blue flowers. She sat by the makeup counter just outside her bathroom.

She put on some basic eye cosmetics. She didn't wear makeup often—she didn't need it in her profession—but she was no fool. Appearances still mattered. She wanted to make sure her face and hair looked perfect, as she was about to call and brag about her victory. Satisfied with her looks, she stood up and hit a button on the side of the table. The mirror extended to the ground as the table split in half and moved out of the way. She thought of who she wanted to contact, and the mirror did the rest, reading her mind and then automatically making all the connections necessary for a call. A picture of Devante displayed as it connected. Thirty seconds later, he appeared.

"Commander?" he inquired

"Kubai has fallen. The planet will be yours, Devante. The generals will be landing soon."

"Did you have any reservations about this? Clones are your people."

Devante was testing with this question, but she was prepared. "None, sir. You know I am devoted to you and your cause. Maybe even more so than yourself, as no child should grow up like I did, forced to be property without having parents to love them."

Devante could see the rage flare in her eyes. Satisfied, he decided not to press the issue. "This cannot be traced to me. This isn't sanctioned by my father, God-Reign. He doesn't mind me conquering the independent planets as long as I don't cause him any political headaches."

"He won't have any reason to worry," Skyfall replied, "as I have followed your instructions. God-Reign will not have any reason to stop our escapades."

"Then victory it is. Return to the *Winter Palace* as soon as you are done there. You deserve a celebration ceremony." Devante reached for the communication device on his end. "By the way, you look lovely today." The call disconnected.

Commander Skyfall felt her white cheeks fill with color. This faded fast, as, being the star commander in his military, she was used to his compliments. It felt good to be on top. Her thoughts returned to the immediate issues. She had to finish what she had started on Kubai. She would need to land on the surface, as she needed a souvenir for her rendezvous with Devante's luxury ship at the *Winter Palace*. She had just conquered a planet; she could not show up empty-handed.

***

Two weeks later

Commander Skyfall arrived at Devante's flotilla. She was shuttled from one of her nameless mercenary ships to the luxury cruiser, the *Winter Palace*. It was a gorgeous ship with gold-plated sides and a giant glass dome with a garden inside decorating its front end. Skyfall arrived at the docking bay, and the doors opened to her grand arrival. Soldiers on both sides saluted her in their dress uniforms. *It's nice to see things back to normal,* Skyfall thought.

Devante greeted the commander, taking her hand and kissing it. She wanted to smack him each time he did that, but this tradition was... well, a tradition.

"Are you sure my clone hands won't kill you?" she joked

Everyone had a quick laugh at this attempt to lighten the mood.

"That's right. Never trust a clone," Scarlet Lilly snapped back, her slanted eyes glaring at Skyfall. Lilly had never liked her. Too bad she was Devante's wife. She should really have been called God Lilly, but Scarlet preferred to be called by her maiden name. That had never sat well with Skyfall.

Skyfall, Devante, and Scarlet were not alone in the docking bay, and it got quite crowded in the halls as she walked past. Various commanders were there, including Mantis, the right-hand man of Dark Reign. This made him one of the highest-ranking officers on the ship, actually, the entire flotilla, as he was second only to Devante here. Devante motioned for Skyfall to follow him as they walked two-by-two down the hall. Eventually, they entered the park in the middle of the dome. She could tell that Devante wanted to speak with her.

"How was your meeting with Baron Bane?" he asked.

"The baron was dead," she replied, "replaced by another criminal named Lord Hate. You know the underworld. If it's not one drug dealing smuggler, it's another."

Devante pointed to the top of the glass dome as indoor fireworks started exploding. Commander Skyfall was quite impressed, as she had never seen such a thing. Devante had truly brought out all the tricks for her this time. Mantis, standing with Scarlet Lilly, applauded, but Scarlet abstained in protest, her racism even more pronounced today. The smoke from the fireworks dissipated quickly because of the extra atmospheric scrubbers that were in place. After the display, the crowd left to go change for the dinner planned in Skyfall's honor. Devante and Skyfall stayed behind to sit on a bench and talk.

"When do I get my ship back?" she asked timidly.

"The *Sky Marshall*? Oh, that is a beauty of destruction. I am sure you are missing the firepower. It is in Mantis's command right now. He has it following my ships. As soon as this clandestine war is over, I will have him give it back to you. The Independent Planets needs to be taken back a notch, and we must stop the advance of the cloners."

Skyfall nodded in agreement.

A young, scantily clad woman entered. "Time to get ready for dinner."

Devante took his leave, but when Skyfall moved to follow, the assistant stopped her. "Scarlet Lilly requests to see you," the young lady explained.

"Tell her to stuff it up her cunt!" Skyfall yelled.

"Commander, it is an order."

Disgruntled, the commander followed the young woman, mumbling obscenities under her breath. "What is your name?" she asked.

"Kayleen," the young woman stated.

"Kayleen, if I ever see you in such a disgrace to the uniform again, I will personally sell you to slavers," Skyfall stated as she entered the chambers of Scarlet Lilly.

Immediately, she was jumped. She tried to fight the big guards, and she put up a good resistance, but they soon overpowered her, mostly because they had surprised her.

"You look better this way, tubey," said Scarlet, making Skyfall growl—she hated the derogatory term for a clone. "I am only going to tell you this once. Stay away from my husband. He doesn't need to soil himself with a tubey like you. I might still want to fuck him every once in a while. I won't want to go within ten feet of him if I have to deal with your sloppy seconds."

"He's too good for scum like you. You don't even understand him or the cause."

"I forgot you are just a good soldier. Don't give me that crap, sister. I know your game. Now, here is what you are going to do. You are going to tell me every time he calls you. Every communication you two make, I want to know about it. Do you understand me?"

Skyfall nodded in agreement. She did not have any choice in the matter right now.

"Freshen up. We don't want you to be late to your own celebration, Commander," Scarlet said, barely able to contain her sarcasm. Then she and her guards left the room.

Skyfall was left to her own devices. There was plenty of makeup to hide her cuts and bruises from the scuffle. She comforted herself with the thought that, someday, Scarlet would have to depend on her. Someday, she would need the military's protection. Then Skyfall could pay her back for this little stunt. But who was she kidding? She wasn't that cruel. She wouldn't harm a hair on Scarlet's body... well, unless Devante demanded it. Skyfall felt that her devotion was pure. Worldly concerns came second to the cause. Done thinking about her wounded pride, she finished covering up her wounds. Then she thanked Scarlet Lilly: this beating had brought her back to reality.

When it was time for dinner, Skyfall left the room with a smile on her face.

# Chapter 10

Chancellor Judy opened the conference, saying, "Welcome to our second session on security and international affairs. If you are here, you should have the highest security clearances only. I ask that all assistants drop off the conference because this is top secret only, ladies and gentlemen."

An officer stood. "Scott Johnson from Intelligence. I have some situation updates for everyone. First off, our efforts with the Galactic Planetary League have been successful. More systems are going to support us in the Galactic Cloning Congress. Second, and this one's important—it's an emergency, actually."

"Let me give you a word of advice," said the chancellor. "Next time, lead with the emergency. Everything else can be sent in a memo."

"Yes, Chancellor."

"So, what is it? We are all here waiting for the information. Spit it out."

"The Acolytes are blaming us for the attack on their homeworld. They have enough fake evidence to declare war on us. Our intelligence suggests that it's just forgeries."

Various officials offered different solutions and the war hawks grumbled their 'I-told-you-so's.

"Listen," said Chancellor Judy, bringing the room to silence, "we can't afford open conflict with the Acolytes. We don't have the resources for a prolonged conflict. We all know the CDF would crumble in the face of such a well-organized enemy. Direct military conflict is not how we win this war. Fortunately for us, our enemy is an empire made up of several different factions. I happen to be well informed that several of these factions are more loyal to their planet than they are to the prince of hate."

The room erupted in laughter. They always loved her favorite nickname for Devante. "I propose you give me the authorization to activate one of our greatest weapons, Agent Snapdragon. She will seek out rogue elements in the Acolytes' government. Then we can divide and conquer. This will make them ripe for regime change to a government with some more agreeable heirs. We will help install a leader who can appreciate our clone products. We can even install Dark Reign as their new leader. He's a military mastermind but a political novice. He will be easy to manipulate. His military focus will keep him looking to crush his own people for some time to come."

This time the conference broke out in applause. Chancellor Judy knew she looked smug and stoic; she always did after a speech.

"Brilliant," said Logan Michaels, the leader of the chancellor's political party. "You have outdone yourself, Chancellor. Regime change is the only answer, and we have the means to do it. God-Reign has sealed his own fate by refusing to deal with his son."

# Chapter 11

"Guards, guards, help! He's dying!" Ninety-eight and Ninety-nine looked at Ninety-six as though he were crazy. They seemed to be wondering why he was standing at the door yelling and pretending to be dying.

"Ninety-six, have you lost your mind?" asked Ninety-eight.

Ninety-six turned and shushed them to avoid ruining his plan. "Guards, quickly!"

"What is going on in there?" they heard one of the guards say.

"Come quickly. I don't know what is wrong with him."

The door opened, and the guards walked into Ninety-six's ambush. They were surprised by his sudden ferocity. He smacked and pelted them until they stopped resisting. His brothers, Ninety-eight and Ninety-nine, helped to inspire his ambition for freedom. They each punched until the guards turned into swollen blood baskets. Blood on their knuckles, blood on the floor, blood on their clothes—it was everywhere.

"Time to leave, brothers," said Ninety-six.

"No, it's not. At least not for us," said Ninety-nine.

"Go. We will clean this up and try to buy you some time," added Ninety-eight.

"Take this." Ninety-nine gave Ninety-six a small drive.

"What's this?"

"It's something that seems very import to the chancellor. Maybe it will give you some leverage if you get captured."

"Thanks, brothers. I won't forget you."

Ninety-six left the room and ventured down the hallway. He kept walking, not truly knowing where to go, until he ran into a janitor. "Hey, you," the clone said, obviously referring to Ninety-six, "if you are looking for an orbital drop, go down the central hallway and take a left."

Ninety-six responded with a look of confusion, but the janitor gave him a wink and carried on with his business. "Thanks, brother" he yelled as he followed the instructions.

He found his way to a staging area. Soldiers were all around him, scurrying about, getting into a large dropship preparing to travel to a battle zone down on the planet. They were all much too busy to notice him and his obvious face tattoo.

"They are really scraping the bottom of the barrel, sending sex clones down to the surface. Who's next, the janitor?" a sergeant proclaimed, and he chuckled at the silliness of the CDF. "Can't even say you are the first I've seen. I just sent an entire squad of you guys down a couple of days ago. Didn't think they were more than laser fodder, though." Ninety-six gave the sergeant a thoughtful look, letting him know that what he had just said was concerning.

"Don't worry. You might not turn out like the others. Go to Drop Pod C17, and you will drop down individually to the urban offense."

Ninety-six gave the sergeant another look of bewilderment. He turned aimlessly, not knowing where to go. He had to make it off the ship, but his chances of survival were now looking slimmer. He wasn't trained in war and had no clue how to get in a drop pod.

"Jeez, they didn't train you at all, did they? Here, takes this gun. Get in this pod," said the sergeant.

Swoop. The pod door slammed shut. Ninety-six gave the sergeant a worried look through the glass, but he didn't seem to care this time. Instead, he gave the glass a hard smack and then waved goodbye as he typed in a launch code.

Ninety-six watched as the *Freedom Fall* faded away into the background and the planet's surface rushed towards him. He clutched the rifle given to him. The sergeant must have turned on a quick basic training program because it started to show on the glass in front of him. It went over how to aim the rifle and how to turn it on. Ninety-six tried to replay the video in his head, as the information came at him fast. *I'm not going to remember any of this*, he thought.

The pod slammed into the ground, and the main window popped open. Blaster fire erupted around him. Clones were dying in front of his eyes, and other pods were landing and descending everywhere. *Here goes nothing*, he thought, and he exited the open pod and entered the battle.

# *Chapter 12*

"How could the Keepers betray me, Skyfall?" asked Devante.

"I'll look into it."

"That's not good enough. The plan is ruined. My reign is ruined, over before it started."

Skyfall moved her weight to her back heel and then crossed her arms. "So, the Keepers are behind it all? Do you want me to punish them? I can organize a fleet within a day."

"We can't. My family will lose the empire. We are not strong enough without the Keepers. What am I going to do?"

"Well, throwing your furniture around and having a fit accomplishes nothing," Skyfall replied.

"I just can't continue without the Keepers. I need their ships, their territory, and their support."

"What if we can use this to our advantage? Make this something good for the cause."

"How so? The investigation is pretty much ruined."

"Not if we change the footage. I have some captured CDF soldiers who would be glad to do anything besides rot in their cells."

"I can't. I owe it to my people to tell them the truth. We have to get vengeance on the real attackers."

"You owe it to the cause to carry out the plan. We are so close. You can't stop now."

"I must."

"No, we must continue. Let me handle this, dear. I can make it all go away."

"Are you sure?"

"Trust me. In no time, we will have our war with CDF and end cloning in the galaxy. Saviors sometimes have to make sacrifices and hard decisions. This is yours." Skyfall drew closer and closer to Devante as he stood there, worried.

"The cause must come first," Devante conceded.

"Yes, it must, and you are its champion."

\*\*\*

God-Reign sat on his throne, sad that his palace in the capital had been destroyed, although he was excited to get a new throne room. This one was much larger and imposing to the onlooker. Not only that, but he'd had the architects remove the history of the rulers from the other families. He no longer thought it necessary to sit in a chair that reminded one about such irrelevant history. The new room praised his father and his ancestors only. It praised them as gods, as they should be.

The room darkened as the war council moved in. It was makeshift and being retrofitted as the new seat of power. The ceiling was being raised, and the walls were being repainted. The representatives of all the powerful houses had come to add their names to the declaration of war that had been brought upon them after the Emortono attacks.

"Great leaders, supporters, and advisors," said God-Reign. "I have brought you together because war has knocked on our door. This is a trying time, one in which we must answer terrorists and feuding governments. This is a time for us to unify, not in war, but in peace. We must be the strongest of all and lead in the face of tragedy. The evidence brought forth proves without a shadow of a doubt that the CDF conspired with terrorists to strike at us. But we cannot blame their citizens for these rogue actions. We cannot be so blind as to run in, guns blazing, on what amounts to nothing more than that. That is why negotiation, preparation, and seeking a peaceful solution are the only ways forward. I will not risk the life of another citizen, because violence will beget nothing but more violence."

Some clapped, while others raged and waved their fists in defiance. The head Keeper remained calm, waiting for the initial reactions to calm. His religious garb clashed greatly against the military-inspired fashions of the rest of the room. "We will pay for the decision you made here. We will pay dearly."

***

Snapdragon looked around until she saw her target. She had to make her move. "Dark Reign, is it?"

He turned, disappointed. "Yes, soldier?"

"Intelligence officer, actually."

"What do you want?"

***

"You can't let this stop you," Skyfall demanded.

"He is our leader," replied Devante. "There is nothing I can do about that."

"Maybe there is. You can't let the cause die on the words of a pacifist."

"I must."

"Fool." Skyfall stormed out of the room.

Devante watched in disbelief. A commander had never been so brave as to just leave without being dismissed, and for his top commander to do so made him stand there in plenty of shock.

*It can't end like this.* Flashbacks of the past filled his mind. He started to think of the atrocities he could prevent that the unnatural and immoral CDF condoned. *I could prevent the enslavement and torture of an entire race of people. There is no way I will just sit idly by while it happens. I'll change his mind. There is something that can change it. I have to do this. There is no other way.*

Devante drank some fresh rum made in his distillery on a lower level. The locals knew how to have fun. *This was the perfect place to open that distillery,* he thought. Exiting his room, he was surprised to see Skyfall waiting for him.

"I knew you'd come around," she said.

# Galactic Mandate: A Radical Cause

"No time to brag, Skyfall. We need to go. We can no longer wait for failed leaders to change course."

# Chapter 13

Devante was awoken mid-slumber by his assistant Kayleen. She moved to wake Scarlet Lilly as well.

"What is this about, Kayleen?" Scarlet grumbled.

"The ship's captain ordered me to summon you. You are needed in the media center, both of you," Kayleen whispered.

Devante got out of bed and put on pants and a sweatshirt, the white of the clothes contrasting with his dark-brown skin. Scarlet Lilly, already in her signature red and yellow pajamas, did not need to change. They followed Kayleen until they reached the media center.

Being a luxury liner, the media center was leaps and bounds nicer for reviewing information than conference rooms on the military ships. It had a holographic projection queued for the center of the room, and recliners lined the walls. Devante liked them because he could see all the commanders of his flotilla around the room. Commander Skyfall sat in the chair to the right of his traditional seat. Mantis sat on the left of Scarlet Lilly. As soon as they took their seats, the captain of the *Winter Palace* started the message.

A news program showed images of the attack on Emortono. It showed images of the cathedral being nuked and of the Shadow Reign being destroyed. The crowd of commanders grew angry and started chattering, their voices joining together to create a low rumble. The captain hushed everyone as he waited for a new transmission to arrive. This transmission was flat and displayed within a glowing box. God-Reign's face appeared, his beard and hair a uniform gray and his skin a little darker than Devante's. Soon, he started to bark orders. "Devante, my son, come to me at the Drake research facility on Nam Tek."

"All the way out there?" Devante asked.

"Yes. Luckily, I was overseeing a project here, so I was not hurt."

The crowd erupted in chatter as they stood up and moved from their seated positions. The captain left to align the ship to Nam Tek and plot a course. Most of the other ships were already doing the same. The commanders rushed back to their assigned ships. As soon as they were all checked, the flotilla could travel through zero space.

Mantis looked down at his virtual tablet. He was receiving orders that had come directly from Dark Reign. Mantis was to return to the *Sky Marshall* and provide protection for God-Reign once he arrived.

Devante turned to Skyfall and said, "Guess you are with me a while longer."

Skyfall's frustration turned into a smile as Scarlet Lilly led Devante away. Within fifteen minutes, they were in zero space and on their way.

***

When the flotilla arrived at Nam Tek, Devante took Skyfall with him, along with his usual detachment of guards. Mantis flew the *Skyfall* in a protective orbit around the planet, reinforcing the flotilla of House Green, which he was the leader of. In total, three fleets surrounded the planet: the Imperial Guard, the fleet of House Green, and Devante's.

Devante landed in the city of Novus, also known as the Raised City. It was supported by giant stilts a hundred feet tall. A strange phenomenon of this planet was that in the spring and fall, the sidewalks would sit just above the water level, while, in the summer, the city stood high above a desert. If you jumped off the edge of a sidewalk, you would fall a hundred feet to your death.

Devante and his escort were transported from the spaceport to an elevator. They moved from one elevator to the next as they descended below the city. They passed through the stilts into the underground labs of the Drake research facility. This lab was shaped like a silo.

"Wait here," Devante commanded as he left to see his father. He had never been to the facility, but most rooms and passages were clearly labeled, so he didn't have any trouble finding his way. He needed to see his father alone, and he didn't want the judging faces of guards bothering him. With all that had happened, he had a lot to talk about with his father. He found two scientists in sterile lab coats, both buried deep in their own work. He asked to be led to God-Reign.

"Yes, he is in the cloning facility," one of the scientists replied. Devante was taken aback. He must not have heard them correctly. He followed until he reached a lab with a clear floor. Underneath, he could see thousands of clones through a clear glass floor. Each clone had their own personal chamber, and the tunnel that they were housed in spiraled down for what looked like a mile or two. From where he stood, he recognized what looked like clones of his brothers, Horus and Ram, in some of the tubes. Devante could barely believe what he was seeing. Looking around, he saw two more clones that were not hooked up to the main system. They were in the center of the room above the glass, in their own chambers. It looked like the scientists had been recently experimenting on them. The name of each clone was posted on its chamber. One was named Variant and the other Fractal. Not very good names, but scientists were never known for artistic naming. Variant had a V tattooed on his forehead, and fractal had an F tattooed on his. It looked silly, and Devante couldn't imagine what their creators had been thinking.

Breaking the awe and wonder Devante was feeling, God-Reign came over and greeted his son with a hug. Devante stood there, emotionless, as he was hugged. The two scientists left the room. With the tension in the air and this kind of royalty, they needed to be anywhere else.

"Welcome, son. This is what I have been working on. I know it is surprising, but this technology will lead us into the future."

# Galactic Mandate: A Radical Cause

"You bigot. How could you? What have you done?" Devante reached for the words to say. For him, this was a betrayal that cut deep, and his mind started to hurt as he contemplated what was going on.

"I have taken your DNA, the DNA from all the great house leaders, my own included, and I have cloned us all," God-Reign stated matter-of-factly. "Here, in the middle of this room, are our first experiments of combination, Variant and Fractal. They are the combined DNA of me, you, Dark Reign, and Mantis. Soon, I will combine more DNA into them from the other great imperial leaders. They will become the best of all of us."

"What you are doing here is an abomination. I cannot let you continue."

Undeterred, God-Reign continued. "You stubborn, delusional boy. I let you dwell in the fantasy of your anti-clone crusade for far too long, I see... Not only do you invade the independent planets, but you have the gall to question me? Your leader! Your GOD! I'm done with your bullshit, Devante. We will join the Galactic Planetary League and the CDF in embracing cloning. I will have a grand clone army for the empire. Just think of it. We can replace the other houses with clones of our own. Then maybe I won't have such an incompetent military that allows my flagship to be destroyed. I have known this day would come, that the others would need to be replaced. I just didn't think it would come so soon."

"This can't be," Devante mumbled to himself.

"Yes, and as punishment for your insolence, I will have you negotiate a treaty with the Conglomerate Republic. We will forgive them for sponsoring the terror attacks to initiate our plans."

All his life, Devante had fought against cloning. The enslavement, the repression, the hopelessness it gave those unfortunate souls. Devante, a champion of the natural born, could not tolerate what he was hearing. He finally understood where some of the empire's technical advances had come from, the ones that had helped him so much in his crusades. He understood why his father had allowed his incursions into independent space. The de-sterilization process, the genetic diversity process, they had all come from this lab. Devante realized he was only a pawn in his father's madness. "Your tyranny ends here," he declared, and he drew his sword.

God-Reign, realizing what this meant, flipped a table to impede Devante's path. Drawing his laser pistol, he shot at Devante, but his son was too quick and had already leaped over the table, knocking God-Reign back. Devante's sword pierced his father's heart.

"Guards," God-Reign mumbled. Devante's sword shot out circular metal teeth that moved in a clockwise direction. The teeth connected with God-Reign's flesh, spraying blood everywhere as his lifeless, twitching body fell to the floor.

When the guards rushed in, Devante took his father's pistol and shot them both. Now three dead men filled the room. Devante moved to a control panel and pushed a button to activate the voice functions of the computer. By this time, alarms were going off, interrupted by intermittent laser fire and the sounds of skirmishing.

"There seems to be an emergency," the computer said. "Displaying emergency options. Please select one."

The panel in front of Devante illuminated. His eyes were drawn to an option that read "Emergency purge: All clones." He had to recite some imperial codes. Below, he could see the tubes illuminate with heat, and then they started dropping to the bottom of the pit below. Even through the thick glass, he could hear the screams of thousands as they burned to death. The clones' pods crashed into each other, and as they broke, they sent clones flying into the air. Devante watched the horrific deaths in detail above the glass floor. A three-minute timer remained on the screen in front of him. It was not much longer until the process would be completed.

Another guard burst in. Panicked and oblivious to Devante's presence, he hid behind a desk. Finally noticing the dead bodies, the guard turned to study the room around him. He locked eyes with Devante just as a burst of light traveled through his head.

# Galactic Mandate: A Radical Cause

The smoke of his cooked flesh filled the air with more death, just as Commander Skyfall entered. She looked over her kill, making sure she had done the job. She tossed a head cooker to Devante, and he looked down at it, horrified. "You have to make sure," she said.

Devante was hovering over the lifeless body of God-Reign when Skyfall came over and pressed down on his shivering hand. They started the quick process of destroying the brain with acid. Devante started to cry as grief and anger overtook him. Skyfall held him close to her bosom as he wept.

She held his head, gently stroking his hair, calming him down from the horror he had just committed. She let go of her cause and concerns for a moment, just long enough to comfort another human.

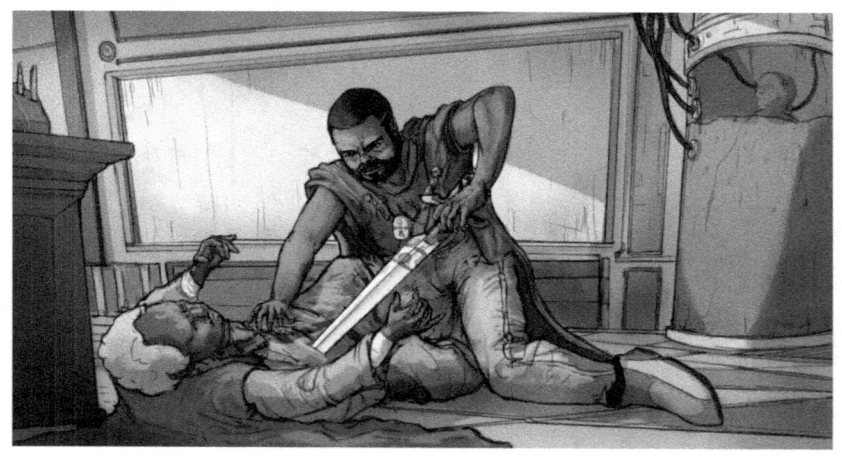

# Chapter 14

So, tell me, clone, why have you come here?" Dark Reign asked.

"To tell you of Devante's treachery, nothing else," Snapdragon replied.

"What intelligence have you gathered?"

"So, you admit you don't have any intelligence."

Dark Reign looked at his guards and nodded. They gave a few quick punches to Snapdragon, a couple across her face and a couple to the stomach. "It doesn't seem like you have anything worthwhile. We should just end it now," he said.

"Wait, we can prove it. We can prove that the recordings Devante presented are forgeries. He never found the true terrorist. Your empire is just as blind as ever." Snapdragon exhaled.

Dark Reign looked defeated. "What does it matter to the CDF? War with you is no longer on the table."

"Let's just say it's a gesture of goodwill for the wars to come," Snapdragon retorted.

Dark Reign drew close to the woman. Her arms were chained to the back of the prison cell, on her knees, surrounded by small puddles of blood. "What wars to come?" he asked.

"The white fleet is still out there, and they are not going to just let you have peace, no matter how big of a pussy your leader is."

At that, Dark Reign was filled with a primal rage. He could not let a slight of that magnitude pass, and he head-butted his prisoner. Snapdragon was knocked unconscious, but it was worth it. A passionate rage filled his veins. Underlings and soldiers moved out of his path, as he bulldozed his way down the hallway to the bridge.

"High alert. Tell the fleet to spread out and seek and destroy. We are going to hunt down the white fleet. All hands on deck. We are doing double shifts until the threat is eliminated."

"Yes, sir," his crew responded in unison.

"Get me the imperial spies. We need to talk."

\*\*\*

Devante stood at the top of the crystal dam wall. It separated an artificial ocean from the desert leading to the ruined immortal city in the background. "Terrorists have killed my father and stuck the Nam Tek. The white fleet continues to terrorize the empire."

The crowd gasped loudly, and the rumbling of chatter. Devante held up his hand to quiet the crowd. "The empire is no longer safe. We cannot sit by while this threat destroys our government one target—one family—at a time. As the rightful heir to God's empire, it is my duty to assume the mantle of God-Wrath. The terrorists and the CDF backers shall feel my wrath, the wrath of an empire!"

Devante, now God-Wrath, brought his hands to his chest and balled them into fists. He grabbed the new crown presented to him and placed it on his head. Instantly, the crowd bowed. Only the leaders of the other houses remained standing with their fists in the air.

God-Wrath pointed behind him, at the ruined capital city, and reminded everyone, "This won't happen again. This is what we will get revenge for. Do you see these refugee camps? Do you see that living grave of a city? That's who we will get revenge for."

\*\*\*

"Devante... I'm sorry, God-Wrath, to what do I owe the pleasure?" Dark Reign asked. The new emperor entered the office of Dark Reign, head of the military. The room was clean with straight lines that came to a head at Dark Reign's desk. The only decoration was the medals he had won during his service. It was a very dark, gray room with black and blue highlights. *These military offices are too bare. There is not enough in them*, thought God-Wrath.

"What a dumb question. War is coming," God-Wrath replied.

"But is it legitimate?" Dark Reign asked.

"Excuse me?" God-Wrath responded.

"I have been uncovering information that the CDF isn't the enemy. They were not the ones who attacked us."

"Who are you loyal to?"

"I'm loyal to the empire," Dark Reign replied.

"Then you will cease this investigation at once. The CDF has been trying to undermine us for a generation. Just because they may not have pulled the trigger doesn't mean that they weren't behind it. I am the empire's wrath, and you will follow my orders."

"I will uphold law and order. I think I know all that I need to."

"Good. I have a mission for the *DKR*. I Need you to order them to Planet Nightshade. I need troops for this war, and the Blood Queen has the best."

"Why not contact them yourself?"

"I am the leader of this empire. I no longer need to command every detail of the military. I'm much too busy for that. You will continue your command over our forces... well, for now. Maybe you are too loyal to a dead man to do your job."

Dark Reign grunted.

\*\*\*

"Queen Siri, glad to open communication with you, although I wish it was under better circumstances," Chancellor Judy greeted smugly from her desk via video chat. The chancellor appeared professional, dressed in a suit. Her business-like appearance stood out from the stone walls of Siri's Palace. Vines ran down the walls, giving the communication room a more natural appearance. The Queen sat across from the large monitor on the opposite wall in one of her many thrones. "I have bad news for you. Our spy in the Acolytes has confirmed that God-Wrath is sending an envoy to invade your planet and replace you with someone more accommodating."

"Let him try. I have the best warriors in the galaxy. EVEN THOSE IN THE BEYOND FEAR MY MIGHT," the Blood Queen replied.

"They do not need to get into a ground war with you. They can just sit in their ships and bomb you back into a back-world outpost."

"We will see about that," the Blood Queen replied.

"Queen Siri, we are detecting two ships coming out of zero space in the system."

"Looks like your time is already up," said the chancellor.

# Chapter 15

The ship and crew of the *DKR*, Kai's new battleship, fired at multiple fighter targets. Alarms sounded, and random screams rang out. The hiss of broken pipes filled the air as unknown white smoke came from them. Five planetary defense orbs targeted the *DKR* for another round of fire. Kai watched in horror on the ship's main viewscreen as the white lights of the defense lasers glowed brighter and brighter.

Just then, a redhead shouted, "The bombers are coming around for a second pass at the orbs!"

Kai frantically replied, "Blow the orbs away, or at least disable them. We can't take too many more hits! Ahhhhhhh!" He was knocked off his feet as the ship rocked from another hit. The orbs had all fired at once, causing a huge shock wave.

"SHIELDS ARE DOWN! ONE MORE HIT AND WE'RE FUCKING DEAD!" an officer screamed.

Kai crawled to his chair. Almost out of breath, he managed to yell, "All missile bays fire everything! Empty the tank!"

Missiles poured from the battleship, and the orbs were overtaken by the furious volley. All five exploded before they could recharge one more time. The bombers acquired a new target, as there were many other ships flying around in the battle.

Finally back in his chair, Kai took a breath, relieved that the defense orbs were gone and the remaining fighters were being shot out of the sky by the gunners and his complement of fighter pilots. His marines were ready, and it was time to give the order for planetary invasion. He pressed a touchscreen button, opening an intercom to the marine bay. "It's time."

Dropships prepared for their launch into space. In minutes, they were gone, heading towards the planet. The outside fighters rallied around them, protecting them from the remaining resistance forces. Twenty ships had departed towards the planet, but ten did not make it, as a white laser destroyed them in a surprise destruction.

"Kai, there is another orb coming from the dark side of the planet. It's rotating towards us. I can see it charging up. We are defenseless. The fighters are gone towards the planet, and we have no more missiles." The officer's report was as grim and dark as his look. He took a flask from underneath his station and guzzled down its contents. "This is it, friends. Nice knowing ya."

The orb drew closer and closer to the *DKR*. *How could I have missed this?* Kai thought. "Where the hell is MANTIS!!!!!!?????" he screamed at the top of his lungs.

As if on cue, Mantis's flagship, the *Hard Prey* jumped in. Unlucky for it, the ship arrived in between the defense laser and the *DKR*, causing it to get hit. Its engines blown out, the *Hard Prey* lost all control and turned left, opposite the direction of the blast. Crashing into the last defense orb, the *Hard Prey* became caught by the gravity of the planet and was pulled down into the atmosphere. Chunks and pieces of the ship flew out into space. A large piece was ripped off by the violent descent, and it collided with the unshielded bridge of the *DKR*, knocking the bridge crew off their feet. The damage was not severe, but it was enough of a jolt to cause injury to some of the crew. Kai found himself lying face-up on the ground.

The *Hard Prey* continued to fall and fall until it finally crashed on the planet's surface.

\*\*\*

Several hours earlier

Commander Kai set foot on his battlecruiser, the *DKR*, just outside of Emortono, where it was waiting with the Mantis battle group.

# Galactic Mandate: A Radical Cause

A strait-laced woman greeted him. "Hello, Commander Kai. My name is Danica, and I will be your new first officer of the *DKR*."

Kai immediately noticed that she was very young, very cute, and very innocent-looking. She must have been right out of the academy because she had the newbie glow. "Danica, show me to the bridge. We must leave this space and head for a planet soon," he requested, a little unsure of himself since she seemed new but had still been on the ship first.

"Of course, Commander."

As they walked through the halls, Kai looked out the windows at the stars. He also could see the flagship of Lord Mantis, who was keeping close to the *DKR*.

Once they were on the bridge, the twelve-man command crew stood at attention. "Back to your stations," Kai barked.

Danica turned to him and said, "I will run the checklist before we leave. The ship will be fully stocked and loaded with ammunition." She shuttled to her station.

Kai's station was obvious: a large chair with an independent computer system overlooking the other stations. Danica's station was not too far away. She was the only one not to have a chair, as she was to stand and be the enforcement on the ship. Kai adjusted to his chair and keyed in the new passwords that he'd gotten from his original commands. Then he stood up and started his first real command.

"Danica, keep running the checklist. Make sure the marines are on board with their special equipment. Then ready the zero drive. We are going to Planet Nightshade."

The crew, even Danica, turned and looked at him with fear and shock. Seeing their horror, Kai knew he had to make a statement. He was the man in charge now, and he thought about how the crew was looking to him for answers and support. But he was a man with a hard upbringing and did not want to sugarcoat it, so he figured he would command with a no-nonsense approach.

"You all heard me correctly. Check the list, set the course, and take us there," he said as Commander Kai, leader of the *DKR*. Feeling pretty highly of himself, he watched the crew get back to work as he sat waiting patiently in his chair. He was secretly terrified, though, by the orders he'd received, and he wondered if anyone could sense his fake confidence.

Danica completed the checklist and moved to the navigation station, hovering over the lieutenant plugging away at the course. She realized she could only get away with this a few times, as the new commander did not know her friendship with Lieutenant Boney. "Boney, did you hear that?" she whispered.

"Yeah, our first mission on this newbie, and we get to go to the only planet with blood warriors," he replied. "We will be fine, but our troops won't."

"Do you have specs on that planet? Maybe it's not as bad as the rumors," Danica whispered even lower in his ear, looking directly at his screen to give the appearance she was micromanaging.

Boney displayed the planetary specs on his monitor. As soon as he did this, Danica's eyes lit up. "This is way worse than I thought. The entire planet is poisoned. Any normal human will die from the air, but the 'Blooden,' as they like to be called, built up immunity. A Darwin effect from generations of living there. In fact, the poison is fully flowing in their bloodstream. The Blooden use this to their advantage, as blood from their wounds kills their enemies in ten minutes."

Commander Kai stared at Danica. He could see her talking, and she seemed to be working, but she must have swayed her attention from the checklist. Excited, fearful, and impatient, he decided to grab her attention. He knew that he was now the boss and he had to act like it every once in a while. "Danica, how far are we on the checklist?"

"Everything is a go. We are just waiting on Mantis."

"Our orders are to jump first, and he will join when his ship is ready," Kai replied.

"Well then, we are ready for the countdown, Commander."

"Set it on the main viewscreen."

"Zero space in five, four, three, two, one..."

# Galactic Mandate: A Radical Cause

***

Present time

When Kai awakened, he was flat on his back, staring up at the bridge's ceiling. He got up and looked around for Danica. He saw her underneath a fallen computer control column, and he rushed over, lifted the column, and woke her so she could get up. She held her lower legs and started rolling around in pain. Kai moved to help her, or at least soothe her since he did not have any medical training, but she waved him away, saying that she would be all right, that she would just suffer through the pain.

Boney, a little drunk, stumbled over. He was perfectly fine since he had been more relaxed when the ship had been hit by debris. "We, uh, gotta move to the lower bridge... you know, the backup. I'll take you there," he said, slurring his words. He did not wait for anyone but immediately headed for an exit, and he was quickly out of sight. Kai got up to follow, but Danica held onto his leg.

"Wait," she said. "He's drunk and going in the wrong direction." She got back on her feet and limped to the opposite side of the bridge. Kai and the other crew members quickly followed her to an elevator in the middle of the ship. It took them down to a more battle-hardened control room. Instead of glass, it had viewscreens to show the outside. The room had a barren, austere look, but everything was sturdier. Danica found her station, and Kai moved to the commander's chair. One of the bridge assistants gave Danica what would have been Boney's chair, as he was still missing and no one knew where he was.

One of the communications viewscreens was blinking, indicating an incoming transmission. A communications officer opened the channel and moved the signal to the main viewscreen. He turned to Kai and announced, "Commander Kai, I'm displaying an incoming distress signal from the *Hard Prey*." Then he went back to work at his station.

A familiar face appeared on the viewscreen, that of Mantis's second-in-command, Kitrrean, and a prerecorded message started to play. *"Hard Prey* to *DKR. Hard Prey* to *DKR.* We need orbital strikes and an...pzzz...team now... We can't hold the blood warriors...pzzz...get your butts down here by order...pzzz."

Kai grabbed his chin, looked at Danica, and gave her what he thought was a smart order. "Danica, order the marines who made it down to the planet to go and rescue Mantis." Kai smiled, feeling sure of himself.

Danica frowned as she looked at her viewscreen. Then she reported, "They are entrenched in the battle for the capital and are requesting backup, which they are not going to get. Protocol demands that we go down with a complement of bodyguards."

"What?? I'm not going down there!"

"Sorry, Commander, but I'm not going to be stuck on this ship if Mantis survives and we didn't make an attempt to help him. He isn't known for his kindness, sir." She started to shake slightly.

"Why can't we just send the remaining marines on the ship?"

"We don't have any more, just crew, and we can't just send a random bunch," Danica replied.

The bodyguards she had been referring to entered the bridge. She had summoned them from her command station while talking to Kai. There were twenty of them, and they stood in two lines.

Kai looked over the muscular guards. "Look at you guys. You don't need me on that planet."

The men replied in unison, "WE GO WHERE YOU GO, SIR!"

Kai just shook his head and said, "FUCK!"

Danica reached for a helmet that one of the bodyguards was holding out to her. She noticed his name was Dex; she would remember him. She had to admit that he had a very defined, rugged face that she really liked. Putting the helmet on, she took another one from him. This one she gave to Kai, as he had now accepted the fact that he had to go. If he didn't, the bodyguards would have to stay, and, well, he would be in deep shit with Dark Reign if Mantis died. Maybe he would be the next person to be publicly hanged, like his friend had been.

Danica smiled at him and said, "The helmets protect against the planet's poisonous atmosphere. Nightshade is not forgiving."

After he put his on, the twenty bodyguards did the same. Then they all headed to the nearest elevator and took it down to the dropship level.

The ceiling of the dropship level was three stories high. Dex moved to the front of the bodyguards, as he was the leader, and faced the commander and the beautiful first officer. She made him nervous. From the way she had looked at him on the bridge, he wondered if there was something there. He could not let his mind get too distracted, though, as the nineteen other guards were staring at him. He took one of the three guns on the gun rack and stood in front of the four remaining dropships. After checking to see if the gun could arm quickly, he began to give the orders everyone was waiting for.

"So, we are going to take two ships down to the planet. There will be plenty of room for us on one, but we will need the firepower of two. Commander Kai and Officer Danica Widow, you two are with me. I'm going to keep you both safe so I don't have to answer to Dark Reign."

Dex pointed to the ten bodyguards standing to his left and assigned them to the other dropship. Raising his gun in the air, he decided on a dramatic finish to his speech. He knew this would be one of his only moments to shine. "For Emortono, for God-Wrath, and for us!"

He turned and leaped over the guardrail, leading the charge of overexcited men to the two dropships. Even the commander and Danica couldn't help but feel the rush as they ran to their assigned ship. Dex found the pilot's chair and immediately started typing in the passcodes to start up the ship. Danica found the first mate's chair and started on communications. Kai, a little lost, strapped into an extra chair to the cockpit, and the guards stayed in the back.

Danica had put on a headset while Kai was not looking, and she seemed to be communicating with someone in a different part of the ship. She turned to look back at Kai and asked, "Can I order one of your bomber squads to escort us down to the planet?"

Kai, a little stunned, just said, "Sure, but why bombers? Why not fighters?"

Danica mumbled a quick reply: "There are none left."

Kai swallowed his spit, looking a lot more concerned than before. Dex let the engine roar, and the dropship lifted off the ground. The other dropship could be seen lifting off as well. Realizing he better give the order before they were on Nightshade, Kai gave a quick nod to Danica.

The ships screamed toward Nightshade, the bombers in formation around the two dropships. For an invasion, things were pretty quiet. The orange atmosphere of Nightshade was strangely eerie, and everyone could tell there was danger all around.

"Fortunately for Mantis, he crashed on a land mass. His shields seem to have cushioned the fall, but the ship is pretty damaged," Dex reported to his commanding officers. Slowly, the *Hard Prey* revealed itself. It was sticking out from between two sand dunes. The few surviving marines of the ship were lined around it. They were quickly losing a battle with the blood warriors. The *Hard Prey* was getting hit by the blood warriors' hovering tanks, but their weaponry was not doing much damage to a ship of that size; however, artillery fire was coming down from somewhere, and it was hitting the ship hard.

The bombers broke off and started defending the dropships as the Bloodens' air force defense reached them. Danica ordered the bomber squad to pull up, and then she decided that she had to act. "Bombers, break off. Take out that artillery. We can defend ourselves," she told the squad leader.

The bombers screamed off, heading in the direction from which the artillery fire was coming. Danica pulled off her headset and gave Dex a direct order: "We need to get on the *Hard Prey* quickly and look for Mantis."

# Galactic Mandate: A Radical Cause

The second dropship was still circling the battlefield, defending the *Hard Prey*. Dex steered his dropship below the other and just above the *Hard Prey*. Then he had the ship's guns shoot a hole in the battleship's hull. He looked back and nodded at Kai and Danica. "Now is the time. Strap on a pack and get the hell out of here."

Kai unbuckled himself and grabbed a jetpack, and Danica did the same. Then Kai, Danica, and the nine security guards strapped on their jetpacks and grabbed assault rifles. One of the bodyguards opened the hatch, and they could see straight down to the ship below. As soon as Danica got her jetpack, on she jumped through the hatch, free-falling down to the *Hard Prey*. Halfway down, her jetpack started up, and Kai watched as she soared down and disappeared into the damaged battleship. The nine guards quickly followed, with Kai in the rear, jumping out and falling into the abyss.

Kai's boots gently landed on the side wall of one of the *Hard Prey*'s halls. The ship had turned sideways when it crashed, so his landing party was walking on the walls while the floors were perpendicular to them. The bodyguards shot at automated defense bots—they were easy to hit, but they were deadly, as one shot from them could rip a man in half. Kai shot randomly and had very little chance of hitting anything. Danica, still leading the pack, found a dark corridor leading straight down, and she jumped in. She was in free fall again, but this time, she stopped in midair when she found a dark hallway with its emergency lights off. Sparks would sporadically light it up, but it was hard to see down it. The bodyguards were right behind her, and Kai was behind them. Standing right near the edge of the corridor, he could see many hallways and cracks in the ship.

Danica noticed two small, glowing green rings. She started to reach for one, but then she heard "Nooo!" and a bodyguard pushed her to the ground. Suddenly, the hall's emergency lights started working again, and in front of her, the glowing rings were revealed: they were not rings at all, but the eyes of a blood warrior.

The bodyguard who pushed Danica to the ground opened fire, his laser weapon squealing, and then the other guards fired as well. The blood warrior was too fast for them, though. His poison daggers penetrated three of the guards, and as the venom interacted with their blood, they started to foam at the mouth and convulse on the ground. One of the other guards, seeing this, threw a grenade. It bounced off the wall, and its red LED countdown started: ten seconds to detonation. The blood warrior grabbed Danica, knocking her on the head, and it was the last thing she remembered.

Kai fell backward as the guards escaped the tunnel that he was standing on the edge of. Falling a story and a half, he was knocked out on impact. Two other guards jumped out as the grenade went off. One of the bodyguards wasn't so lucky. Catching the full blast of the grenade, he was blasted into nothingness. The hallway collapsed. A bodyguard fell flat on his face, the blood spilling from his chest and covering the floor next to Kai. The four remaining bodyguards floated in the open space of the ship, their jetpacks having saved them from the grenade. They landed next to Kai, looking over his lifeless body and wondering if he had survived.

\*\*\*

When Danica awoke, she was being dragged by her hair. She could see nothing but emergency lights dimly flashing in the dark. Finally, she was dropped in the middle of seven other blood warriors. Spun around and now facing the warriors, she scurried backward in terror. The warrior who had captured her was the only one with his face showing. The rest wore plain, rusted masks that covered the lower halves of their faces. It was a scary sight for her. She wondered what their intentions were, and she feared she would be raped, murdered, or tortured. She didn't know what they would do; maybe they would do it all to her.

"What are you going to do to me?" she dared to ask. Her red hair tousled, her body aching, her makeup running down her face, she looked a mess, but she was still extremely attractive to the men standing around her. Her look was common among women of that planet, but most were not as attractive as Danica.

Her captor came forward, taking a green vile from his vest. He rubbed the ooze into his skin and then immediately used his other hand to scoop it up and place it on Danica's exposed skin. She tried to resist, but a warrior from behind her grabbed her by the hair and suspended her in the air.

Her skin began to burn. They continued to hold her in the air, waiting for the reaction. Slowly, the burning spread to cover more and more of her skin. She started to feel like she was on fire, but she could only struggle and moan. She had no way to cool down, but she waved her arms to cool them. That is when she got a swift punch to the back, and the warrior let go of her hair, sending her falling to the floor.

Her captor started to speak, but she interrupted him with a wailing moan. "Ahhh, what have you done? Make it stop." Her whole body burned, even in places she didn't know she could feel.

Her captor bent down and looked her in her crying eyes. "Where is Mantis?" he asked.

"I don't know!" she cried out.

The blood warrior's eyes glowed, but only for a few seconds. The pain grew, and she realized that somehow, the blood warrior had control of it.

"Where is he?" the blood warrior demanded. This time, his eyes glowed for a full minute.

"I don't know. I didn't come with him. I came with Commander Kai," she whispered in agony.

"Is he an Acolyte lord?" This time, he dimmed the pain with his eyes, knowing that she could not take much more.

"No!" she cried.

"Hmm," interjected one of the blood warrior's masked companions. "We should hunt him down and kill him anyways. Killing commanders always demoralize the enemy."

Her captor nodded, and then he signaled three warriors to hunt down Commander Kai.

"Back to where we were." The captor's eyes glowed again, raising her pain back to intense levels. Danica didn't know if she could handle it. She felt life itself start to fade from her body. "Where is Mantis?"

\*\*\*

Kai got up and saw the bodyguards standing around. *These guys are worthless*, he thought. This led to more thoughts of how everything was not going to plan and how this easy bombardment of the planet hadn't turned out so well. He started to think more on what had been in his mission briefing. "Only light planet defenses, they said," he muttered to himself. None of the bodyguards heard him, especially after the loud blast. *Mantis said this would be easy, that we would just convince the queen to ally with us. We just had to make sure we didn't land on Nightshade, because they are vicious.* Kai couldn't believe what Mantis had told him before they'd left. But that was what he'd said, and now Kai was standing in the middle of a wrecked ship.

The bodyguards moved toward him, and Kai suddenly realized he was the man in charge. They had two choices: they could find Danica or find Mantis, and if they didn't find Mantis, Kai would be as good as dead. "Guards, let's find the battle bridge. I think Mantis will be there," he ordered.

A guard looked at him questioningly. "What about Danica, sir? They took her."

Kai still wasn't getting the respect or the unquestioning loyalty that the experienced commanders did because of how new he was. He turned to the guards, having a mild panic attack, and yelled, "We've got to find Mantis NOW! Dark Reign will have our heads if we don't! Don't give me any more lip! We have to go, and we have to go now!!!"

\*\*\*

Dozens of small praying mantises scurried across the steel floor, making small hisses that were very distinguishable. The small, nano-controlled beings crawled onto the two unsuspecting blood warriors who were interrogating Danica. They clawed and bit into the warriors' skin, eating through their organs. They crawled underneath their armor and masks. The blood warriors fought, trying to punch, kick, and slap the little bugs off, but they quickly lost the battle as soon as the small mantises started to eat vital organs. Blood and guts were smeared over their tiny mouths, which were now foaming. Their evil eyes were still hungry for another victim besides the two lying on the floor, but even the small bugs were not immune to the poison that ran through the warriors' blood, and they started to twitch and shake, most not even making it out of the bodies before dying violently.

The other warriors stood in battle-ready formation, readying their heat pistols so that they would not fall victim to the same fate. They looked around, trying to find the source of the bugs.

An armored figure appeared, one unique among the Sierra Advent. The armor's light-green color closely matched the light beige and green of the blood warriors' attire. Danica was relieved at the sight of him, recognizing this figure as Mantis. Only he could have been responsible for the ill fate of the fallen warriors. On Mantis's torso was his unique, V-shaped armor, made of a hard-composite metal. He also wore bracers and grieves of the same material. The bracers had a spring-loaded, fork-like weapon that he could shoot or stab with.

The blood warriors fired their heat guns, but they had no effect on Lord Mantis's armor. Shooting his metal forks, Mantis made quick work of the blood warriors. Soon, only Danica's captor remained. He dropped his heat gun, pulled out a dagger, and charged Mantis, who easily blocked the attack. Mantis grabbed the last warrior by the throat, and he watched him struggle for his life. "Aah...huuhhh." He twitched and squirmed until Mantis flexed the muscles of his hand, snapping the blood warrior's neck.

Danica looked up at her savior. Still in pain, she slowly got up and moved towards him. "Thank you so much for—" Danica started to say, but she was interrupted by a backhand from Mantis. In her weakened state, she lost consciousness, but at least the pain was gone.

*\*\**

Kai and his bodyguards flew through the ship, searching the halls as they made their way deeper into the ship. It wasn't as damaged deep inside. One of the bodyguards knew the layout from a tour of the ship he'd taken before. Eventually, they found themselves in front of a locked elevator shaft.

"This is it," the bodyguard said.

"Good job," Kai said approvingly. "What is your name?"

"I'm Cebo," the guard replied proudly. He started prying the door open, and the other guards helped. With their combined might and knowhow, they opened the doors, revealing the empty elevator shaft beyond.

"We must go up there, and we will find the door for the battle bridge," Cebo said.

"Won't the bridge be locked, too?" another guard asked.

Cebo jumped into the shaft, telling the other guard, "No, Mantis never locked the bridge. Guy thinks he's too much of a badass to be touched."

Kai interrupted. "Hopefully, he is, because I don't want to be hung."

Quickly, Kai followed Cebo and the others down the hallway. A bodyguard shouted, "I've got the back," and he tried to close the elevator door, but it wouldn't shut. The other guards followed Cebo and Kai up the shaft, slowly moving in a space that was not meant for people to travel quickly.

Kai looked back and then asked Cebo, "So, who is that in the back?"

"That's Dread. He's our best marksman. I wouldn't worry with him behind us."

The group traveled for about fifteen minutes up the shaft, and then Cebo told everyone to be quiet. "I think I hear something."

Dread heard it too. He stared behind them, as he had done the entire time.

A communicator on Kai's arm buzzed. "Kai, this is Dex. Are my brothers, Lex and Rex, with you?"

A dagger, dripping with so much acid that it was being eaten through, flew past Dread's face. Then three sets of glowing green eyes appeared. The blood warriors who had been sent after Kai had finally found him, and it had been his communicator that had given them confirmation.

Dread screamed in pain as the acid dripped on his face. He popped off a shot as he fell back to avoid the dagger. Luckily, the shot caught the blood warrior on the left, killing him instantly. Kai fired indiscriminately, hitting just about everything but the blood warriors in front of him. Lex and Rex, who were standing on either side of the room, charged forward, taking the blood warriors by surprise. Kai stopped firing so as not to hit his own men, taking this as a good moment to reload.

Lex attacked a blood warrior, using his gun more like a bat than what it was intended for. Unfortunately, the blood warrior was prepared, and he spun out of the way, tripping Lex, making him fall on his face. The blood warrior looked down at Lex, about to stab him with his weapon, when his head exploded. Cebo had him in his sights and was not about to let another comrade die.

Rex was in a fistfight with the other warrior. He was also using his gun like a club, but unlike his brother, he was connecting with his blows, wounding the blood warrior. Eventually, Rex clubbed the warrior's head so hard it broke the man's neck.

Dread got up. He was hurting, but it was nothing compared to what he'd gone through before. He ran up to Lex and asked, "Are you ok? Did you get any of the blood on your skin?"

"No," Lex replied, looking directly at the nasty burns on Dread's face, "but I'm surprised you're the one who's asking."

Rex helped his brother up, and they all continued their journey up the shaft. They were proud of their accomplishment, realizing that they'd just taken out three blood warriors—a feat that made them some of the toughest warriors in the galaxy.

Cebo led them up until they reached a red door. It was sideways to the direction they were moving, and it had a small window in it. They could see Mantis on the other side, in a room full of people. Kai shouted, "Finally!" and he kicked open the door and jumped into the room.

Cebo reached for him, shouting, "Nooo!" and then he was forced to follow. The others jumped into the room as well.

\*\*\*

Danica screamed and again awoke to pain. This time, it was a whip across her back. She looked around, and a female figure appeared. "Did that hurt, baby? Don't worry, there will be plenty of time for that later," Kitrrean said to her before she started to scream. Mantis had touched a button on his belt, sending terrible electric shocks through both women.

"Settle down, bitches," he said.

Danica rose to her feet, saying in agony, "How do you get away with this?"

Mantis touched the button on his belt, but for only a second. "I said settle," he commanded.

Both Kitrrean and Danica faced Mantis, saying in unison, "Sorry, Lord Mantis."

"Now, that is better."

Just then, Kai and his bodyguards dropped in. Kai tried to approach Mantis, but then the lord touched his belt one last time, forcing the commander and his bodyguards to bow down in pain. Kai screamed out, "This is how you treat your rescue party?"

"Please, you're just the ride," Mantis shot back.

"Huh?"

"This ship does not have any terrestrial transport and is obviously out of commission itself, and I have to be in the capital soon," Mantis explained. He motioned for everyone in the room to rise, since he needed to explain his plans to them. Pacing the room, he began to let the others in on the plan.

"How are we to conquer this planet if our battleships are toast and we don't have enough soldiers to even occupy a city?" Kai interjected fearfully, as he did not want to be in any more pain at the hands of Mantis.

"There is a regiment of rebels waiting for us in the capital. Once we reach them, we shall run a coup on the Blood Queen. Kai, what condition is your ship in? I know it's not toasted like you say, since I took quite a hit and you wouldn't be here if it were."

Kai looked at Mantis, a little uneasy. He had almost gotten used to not having any superiors around. "It took a beating. We were out of ammo, so I don't know what use it could be."

Mantis turned his attention to Kai once more. "You're not thinking like a commander. No wonder Dark Reign left me in charge of this. If it were up to me, I would still have you guarding the border. Order your ship to fly down to the surface and hover above the capital. As long as we can get the Blood Queen to surrender before I kill her, her followers will accept the rebel's rule."

Danica let her tongue slip, and she asked, "So, we are bluffing?"

Mantis turned his head quickly to look at her, hovering his fingers about his belt. "Yes, we are, but if the queen's army resists, then we have wasted our time here. We need these warriors to serve me as we get vengeance for our homeworld. They will be the foot soldiers for our powerful armada. Have you not read your mission logs, officer? What are you doing as second in command if you can't understand the stakes?"

Danica knew not to answer—well, at least as long as he had his fingers above his belt.

Mantis now moved behind Kitrrean, getting uncomfortably close to her. Kitrrean wished she could just turn around and smack him in the face, but she had done it before, and Mantis hadn't liked it very much. Kitrrean liked being the aggressive one when it came to men, and sometimes, she could handle a strong man who could stand up to her, but something about Mantis made her skin crawl. She did not like how he never seemed soft and he always seemed fed up with everything. Ever since she had been transferred to his ship, Mantis had shown an unusual liking to her, but she just wished she could get away. Showing weakness was not what Kitrrean was about, so she avoided Mantis—an easy task on a full ship, but much harder now that most of the crew was dead.

Mantis whispered in her ear as he pressed the electrical shock button, and the others in the room looked away, as they did not want to be the next targets. Kitrrean fell to the floor in pain from the shock, glad that she could not move away from Mantis. He moved closer to Danica and whispered in her ear as well, shocking her at the same time just as he had just done with Kitrrean.

Kitrrean stood, walked up to Kai and his bodyguards, and announced, "Mantis is tired of talking and wants to kill instead, so Kai, we need you to call your transport. It's time to get off this ship and head for the capital."

Kai turned on his communicator and called up Dex. "Dex, we got Mantis, so get the dropships here. We are heading for the capital."

Mantis whispered in Danica's ear, "I need you to kill as many blood warriors as you can. I'm not gonna give you any slack because you're a woman."

Danica was shocked, figuratively this time, and amazed; she had never heard such disrespect in her life. Making a funny face, she moved away. She did not have the fear of those who had been around him for a long time. But she was learning that he had way too much fun inflicting pain on his officers.

"I'm in position!" Dex's voice shouted from Kai's communicator.

With that, Mantis strapped on a jetpack and opened a hidden release hatch that went from the bridge to the outside. Getting a running start, he turned on the pack and jetted out of the ship.

Kai and his guards already had their jetpacks on, and they ran toward the circular tunnel that Mantis had left from. Soon, Kitrrean and Danica had put on their packs as well, and they followed the others out of the tunnel. As they came out, they could see the dropship, and the bay doors were open, so they landed in the ship.

# Galactic Mandate: A Radical Cause

The dropship flew toward the capital city as their bomber escort joined them. Lord Mantis gave Dex the coordinates of the rebel fighters. The group was set to meet these rebels outside the gates of the Blood Palace of the Blood Queen.

***

Two hours later, they approached the Blood Palace. They'd had enough time for a good meal and some energy drinks, which were designed to give them lasting energy for the many battles ahead.

Mantis was using a control panel to make a scan of the Blood Palace. Loading this into the circuitry of his body armor, he now had a map of the full structure. Zooming in on a portion of the map, he waved for Danica. "Tell the bombers to strike the south side of the palace. I want an opening for us to jump into."

Danica moved to her station and completed the command immediately. Kai looked around, wondering what was next, but he did not have to wonder for long as Mantis gave his second order. "Get your jetpacks back on. We are all jumping down as soon as the palace is struck."

They heard a small boom followed by several louder ones. Dex hovered above the hole in the palace, opening the bay doors for them to jump back into action. The members of the group leaped out of the ship in no apparent order. Eventually, only Dex, Lex, and Rex were left. They were preparing to jump together when the ship was hit by one of the palace defenses. The hit caused Dex and Lex to fall from the ship, and they looked back in horror to see that Rex had not been as lucky as them. He was standing in front of oxygen tanks at the moment they exploded. Dex and Lex heard nothing but burning as they saw all the flesh of their brother incinerate away.

On the ground, Mantis motioned the group to quickly follow him. He knew the queen's guard would be coming quickly. Even he could not take on that many well-trained men at once. "We must go down to the septic rooms. That is where the rebels are meeting us," he explained.

Dex and Lex landed with tears in their eyes. Kai looked at them, and then he saw the burning ship falling onto a different part of the city. He did not ask what had happened to Rex, as he already knew. "This way, quickly. The palace guard will be on us at any moment," Kai yelled at them to get them back into reality.

The group followed Mantis down hallways and stairs, towards loud sounds of fighting. They heard the screams of warriors and knew they were heading in the right direction. Suddenly, they heard a high-pitched beeping. Then there was an explosion, and the wall right next to them collapsed. The queen's guard had found them.

Their glowing eyes could be seen in the darkness of the gaping hole in the wall. Poison daggers flew towards Dread, but Cebo tackled him before they hit. Mantis looked at Danica and Kitrrean, folding his arms to make it fully known that he was not going to help out in this battle. The girls grabbed their guns and pointed them at the hole in the wall.

Kai screamed, "Let's get the hell out of here!" and he led his guards past Mantis, wildly shooting behind him. The women provided cover fire as they vacated the area. Danica threw all three of the grenades she was carrying behind the group in an effort to buy them some time. Daggers zoomed past, coming very close to hitting them. Then an explosion collapsed more of the building around them. They picked up their pace and ran towards the septic tanks. Mantis led them to a door, which he tapped on in an odd pattern. They entered after hearing a similar knocking pattern from the other side of the door.

Inside, they were welcomed by a group of barbaric-looking men. "You have made it. I was beginning to doubt you, Mantis," the muscular leader said. The group waited for Mantis's response.

"Whatever," he fired back. "I'm here to help you overthrow the queen." Mantis was never one for pleasant meetings.

"And just how do you plan to help?" asked the leader. "There aren't many of you left."

"We will force the queen to surrender," Mantis explained. "First, we will go capture her. Then our mighty battleship will fly over and squash any resistance."

The leader studied Mantis. He could see how mighty Mantis could be. The fact that he did not have fear made him someone to be taken seriously. "We will get you past the elite royal guards, and we will see."

The group found themselves listening to the screams of dead warriors as they followed the rebels through the catacombs of the palace. The rebels blasted through a door, creating an opening to a large throne room. The rebels motioned for the group to go through the opening, but facing resistance from the royal guard, they could not follow.

Once inside, the group checked the corners and around the room in an attempt to secure it. From the other side of the hall, blood warriors began firing lasers at them. Danica hid while Kitrrean covered her. Mantis decided to hide as well, taking his time and waiting for his opportunity to strike. Kai and his remaining bodyguards, Dex, Lex, and Cebo, were the only ones firing at the enemy.

Mantis came out from hiding and ran over to the ladies, who were crouching in a corner of the room. He dropped to the ground and punched the floor next to them, causing a huge bang. Danica and Kitrrean looked at Mantis, shocked, as he grabbed them both by the necks, exposing both to the blood warriors. Mantis had only one thing to say to them: "Kill." Then he threw them onto the battlefield. Quickly, they turned, grabbed their guns, and charged. They ran into a wall of laser fire, barely dodging it. Kai and his guards provided cover, but they were far behind.

They heard growls and barks from across the hall. Dogs had been let loose, and they charged the group. When Kai saw the vicious-looking dogs with foam coming from their mouths, he ran.

"Don't! We'll get separated," Cebo warned, but it was too late; Kai had already knocked into Danica and Kitrrean. They all stumbled through a reinforced door that closed behind them. Cebo and the other bodyguards knocked on the door.

They tried to blast it with their rifles, but they didn't even cause a dent. The dogs grew near and started to circle the bodyguards.

"We have to go," said Lex.

"But the commander is in there," said Cebo. They could hear the stomping of more warriors coming their way.

"If we stay here, the Blooden will surround us. We won't be of any use to the commander dead," said Lex.

"If he is still alive," said Dex. "I'm calling it. We did all we could. Let's get out of here before they make us names on a wall."

Dex and Lex took off, sprinting down the hallways of the palace. Cebo looked back at the undamaged door. He realized there was nothing he could think of doing that would help his commander's situation. He'd told him not to run. Then he ran in the same direction as the others.

Kai looked up and realized that they had stumbled into the spot where the blood warriors were taking cover. A rumbling started, and the floor started to shift as the Blood Queen rose from underneath them. The battle was over. They had been captured by the queen and a swarm of her guards.

# Chapter 16

The throne room of the Blood Queen dripped with the red blood of conquered enemies. Mixed into a more sustainable and sanitary liquid form, but keeping its consistency and most of its properties, it flowed into small fountain pools in the throne room.

The queen's guard emerged from the floor in droves. They had no problem overrunning the small insurgent group led by Mantis and Kai. The team dropped their weapons and allowed themselves to be searched for equipment and technology that could be used against the Blooden.

"Looks like your plan has failed. Your mighty empire is no match for my soldiers. Well, except for one of you." The Blood Queen looked directly at Mantis, watching as he was stripped of his armor. Once bare, Mantis was revealed to be weak, his muscles having atrophied from overreliance on his armor. The smile on the queen's face was replaced with disappointment. She frowned and took a breath, soaking in the copper smell of the room. "Lock them up, all except that one." She pointed at Kitrrean.

The floor opened, and they dropped down into the palace on the same elevator that had risen with the queen when she had made her entrance. The blood warriors took Kai and his team and placed them in a dungeon below the palace.

In the throne room, the warriors shackled Kitrrean. She began to breathe heavily, nervous about what was going to happen to her. She hoped they would allow her to keep her breathing apparatus. She knew that if they removed it, she would die from the poison that the Blooden had so proudly adapted to. She thought about begging. *No, that's not me.* She thought about becoming a traitor, but she didn't have anything of value to offer. She realized that at this point, all her options were exhausted. The only thing she could do was stand in front of the Blood Queen and accept her fate. She arched her back and stood as tall as her restraints would allow.

"We have a brave soul here, gentlemen," the queen said. "This will make ceremony all the better. There is a Blooden tradition when we defeat our enemies called the Rain Ceremony. Have you heard of it?" The Blood Queen raised two fingers, summoning her men to Kitrrean's side. "You really should study the culture of the people you wish to conquer. Maybe then you wouldn't find yourself in such a situation."

Kitrrean shifted her shoulders and kicked as the guards grabbed both her legs and hands. Stretching out, she lay flat, wiggling and squirming, trying to resist the guards as much as she could. Soon, they lifted her up and over the Blood Queen, attaching her shackles to hooks that hung over the queen's throne. They moved to each side, pulling on the ropes, raising her even higher.

Gone was the squirming from before. Kitrrean's eyes wandered in fear. She stared down at the Blood Queen, who now occupied the throne below her. The queen had removed her clothes and was naked except for a small bra and thin underpants. Kitrrean still had her breathing apparatus, but her confidence had faded.

"Are you ready, my queen?" one of the guards asked. Happy that this prisoner was securely stuck in her position, they awaited their next orders.

"Get the priest," she commanded, and the soldiers obeyed.

Moments later, the head priest, Ernie, walked in with a camera crew. "A show of force, my queen," he said. He was draped in highly decorative robes in the traditional Blooden colors of bright green and blood-red accents. He smelled of wealth, and his well-manicured nails matched his regal look.

Kitrrean stared in wonder. She wanted to scream but couldn't because of the large gag in her mouth. All she could do was watch and listen, so she took the advice of the Blood Queen and tried to learn a little bit about their culture, hoping there was some challenge, some move or sound she could make, that would change her circumstances.

"Any luck on finding a husband?" Ernie asked with a half-grin. "Our people will never accept a clone, and you need to marry into strength."

"Even when my rule is challenged by usurpers, you have to bring up this trivial matchmaking game of yours?" the Blood Queen asked.

"It is no game. You must get married and produce heirs so that the worlds can be stable. With the CDF and the Acolytes bringing peril to the galaxy, to our homes, now is a perfect time for a royal wedding. It will strengthen your support among the people. End all this petty rebellion and make you a legend. Think about it. If you get a husband with a navy, that could make us a major player or even a force to be reckoned with. Not just mercenaries for the powers that be."

"One of the invaders was handsome and a warrior, but I found out his strength was just due to a technical aid. He was nothing without his armor. Just like you are nothing without your robes."

"That's not what you used to tell me," Ernie replied.

"Enough. Get on with the ceremony. Start your cameras."

He nodded and sent the camera crew across the room to set up their broadcast. He looked around the room and nodded again. More followers in robes flooded in and lined the walls. Some had bowls, which they filled with blood from the pools. Then they brought the bowls to their chests and waited patiently. "I shall bless you officially this time," Ernie said with a grin. His golden skin seemed to glow in contrast to his hazel eyes. He lowered his hood to reveal the thick, curly hair that stood in a ball on his head. "From the first enemy to the last enemy!" he yelled, and his followers repeated his words, raising their ceramic bowls in support.

Kitrrean started to squirm again, her calmness shattered by the creepiness of the full room. She tried to move and make noises, anything so the people below her would stop acting like this was normal. They didn't seem fazed at all that someone was shackled and suspended above them. Whatever this ceremony was, Kitrrean wanted no part in it. The hooks were surprisingly simple, and she started to think that if she could just wiggle enough, she could break free. The queen would break her fall, and at this point, that could only be considered a bonus. Hopefully, her bones would not break in the process.

"Okay, you are live. The planet is watching," the cameramen said.

*I have to hurry,* Kitrrean thought, and her wiggling grew frantic. *Whatever they are going to do, they are going to do it soon.*

"From the first enemy to the last enemy," they all chanted below her. Ernie held an oddly big blue button. It contrasted with all the red in the room. He waved it at Kitrrean, locking eyes with her while the Blood Queen looked up and tried to do the same. This made Kitrrean pause for just a second. Ernie clicked the button and then sighed as giant metal blades dropped from the ceiling and sliced Kitrrean open.

She hung in shock as her blood dripped onto the queen below. Still aware, she watched as the woman below rejoiced in being covered in blood, her blood. Blood drenched the queen's exposed thighs, arms, and midsection. It seemed to merge with her undergarments, which had been designed to match the look of blood.

"I don't think she needs her mask anymore," the queen said. One of her guards removed his traditional hooked blade from his belt and hurled it at the tube supplying breathable air to Kitrrean, slicing it in two.

Kitrrean was already shaking from the swinging blades that were still draining her of her vital fluids. She started to foam at the mouth, and then a full-on seizure ended her life. Bucking, she rattled her restraints, stretching them until they snapped.

# Chapter 17

"I can no longer rely on our allies. The God's empire must unite on its own. No more fancy politics, Skyfall," God-Wrath said. He was sitting on his father's throne, gazing on a marvel of the galaxy—at least, that was what the broadcast was calling it—the new ship being created from the combination of his old ship, *Winter Palace*, and God-Reign's *Angelic Mist*. Skyfall was silent; ever since the plan had started to come together, she had been more reserved in anticipation of what was to come.

"Skyfall, I am excited. We are finally coming to the end of the cause. All those years of preparation and leaving and trying to make this happen are finally over. With the power of being the God, I can finally rule this galaxy and show it the moral way. The way to the future."

"Yes, my lord... I mean, God-Wrath," Skyfall corrected. "My benevolent leader. It is time to unite, as you said. The camera crews are ready. You may be the greatest ruler we have ever seen." She gestured to the throne room, which was filled with the leaders of all the families. God-Wrath stood in full traditional attire instead of his usual military-inspired clothes, and he looked like a priest.

"It is time we unite as an empire to define our way of life. No longer will we rely on the weak and petty factions to protect us. We will become one, and I call upon all Acolytes from all corners of the galaxy. We need you now. I, God-Wrath, am watching. All those who do not honor my father's memory and commit troops to the war will be labeled traitors and will feel the same wrath that the CDF has coming to it."

"But that will bankrupt us," said one of the family heads.

"Don't worry. The expanse of our borders will pay for any problems."

"This is irresponsible. You will stretch us too thin."

"We can't support this," said another leader. "The human cost will be too great. Think of all the lives we will lose."

"Enough. Pacificism died with my father. We will sacrifice. We will survive, and we will conquer. I order you all to comply," God-Wrath said.

"What about the Blood Queen? She blew up one of our ships. That cannot be tolerated."

"She will be dealt with later. First, we destroy our rivals, the CDF."

"Down with the CDF!" Skyfall interjected. "Down with the CDF!"

The leaders started to follow her lead. "Down with the CDF!"

\*\*\*

Ninety-six ran towards the city. All he could see were bombs being dropped and soldiers fighting. But there was something else: a group of civilians appeared to be guarded by an elite team. With ease, they killed any armed clone that came near.

Ninety-six dropped his weapon. *No use dying for a rifle.* He grabbed some clothes from the body of what looked to be a man about his age. He then got in line with the other civilians. The building they were being rushed into had a large pink sign that read "Brother." *I wonder what that is. It must be some kind of hotel.* They were herded into a large, circular room. Suddenly, it felt like the entire floor was moving—the room was a large elevator. As it moved down, at each floor, they picked up more and more scantily clad women. Finally, the elevator seemed too full to fit anyone else. Ninety-six was obviously mistaken, though, because they fit more and more, cramming everyone into the space.

Eventually, Ninety-six bumped into one of the elite guards. His face was uncovered for just a second, but that was just enough for the guard to notice. "A male pleasure clone tattoo," he said.

"What's a pleasure clone?" one of the many little boys asked. Ninety-six thought it was funny that there seemed to be an endless stream of little boys on the elevator but not little girls. It was very different from where he had come from. The planets he'd visited with the chancellor were usually a lot more balanced than this one.

"Nothing for you to be concerned about, little kid," the guard said, and then, to Ninety-six, he ordered, "Put your hands up. Looks like I caught a spy."

Fathers rushed over to grab their children as they embraced their nannies. Ninety-six surrendered. He was not looking for any trouble. He just hoped he wasn't taken back to the chancellor, though that seemed unlikely with the hostilities going on around them.

The elevator completed its descent into what, because it was so different, must have been a secret level. It wasn't labeled, and it was bare, made out of concrete and not lavish and feminized like the others. It was cold and dirty. The civilians were guided into a large barracks. There, the guards handcuffed Ninety-six and then rushed him into a private room where the sultan waited for him. Along the way, they passed grinders and wired mechanical equipment. They also went past what seemed to be a robotics lab filled with strange conveyor belts. They passed a maternity ward, and then they went into the sultan's private bunker, which was just for him and his elite guard.

"So, they sent you to spy on us?" the sultan said. "Tell me, did you give up our position? What is the CDF waiting for? When will they storm our bunker?"

"I'm not with the CDF. Please, I'm only seeking a safe place." The room broke out in laughter.

"Well," said the sultan, "either you're the worst spy they have, or you are the dumbest sex slave I have ever seen. I don't know how we got defeated by such idiotic people. They didn't send the right gender for a spy anyway. There aren't any male sex slaves on this planet. Well, maybe if you count the in-between kind."

The guard on the left gave a little smile, and the sultan gave him a nasty look. "Stop smiling, Farid. I know the ladyboys are your favorite."

Ninety-six pulled the capsule from his clothes and presented it to the sultan. "Please, let me stay here. I'm not a spy, but I do have something that the CDF wants. It's important, and it came from the chancellor herself," he begged, his face pleading.

"Maybe you are a spy. But you are a spy for me," the sultan said as he handed the capsule to one of his guards. No words were exchanged, but the look of approval from the sultan was unmistakable. There was a waiting period as everyone anticipated the results from the capsule.

The guard, a well-trained man, happily dropped his stoic demeanor to show his sheer glee upon analyzing the capsule. "It's instructions on how to track the white fleet's position. The Acolytes will pay a fortune for this. We are saved."

"We will get asylum and a new planet for sure," the sultan added.

*** 

Admiral Lee sat in his command chair. They had been hiding and studying their targets for weeks. "We have lost our momentum. We need to press the attack, get the Acolytes off balance and on the defensive again."

"I couldn't agree with you more," his lieutenant said.

"What about our contact in the Acolytes? Has she given us any more codes?"

"No, sir."

"What about our contact in the CDF? Have they provided any more intelligence?"

"No, they have not. Everyone has gone silent. I'm afraid we are on our own."

# Galactic Mandate: A Radical Cause

"Then we will go it alone," Admiral Lee declared. "Split the fleet into nuclear assault ships with escorts. Let's hit all fourteen targets at once. They won't see this coming."

The fleet moved into position, and they all engaged their zero drives to reach their very separate destinations.

\*\*\*

"Sir, the sultan of VFA-T10 has called," Dark Reign's assistant said. "He has been trying to contact God-Wrath about some matter of grave military importance."

"Put him through. God-Wrath no longer wants to handle the day-to-day operations of the military, as he so wonderfully stated to me earlier."

"Yes, sir." The assistant saluted, and then she left the room. Moments later, a very desperate-looking sultan appeared on the monitor.

"What do you have for me?" asked Dark Reign.

"Something very important. Something you will give me asylum for."

"Well, it better be worth a lot if you think I will give you anything. I can't imagine what waste of time you have in store for me right now. Just make it quick. I have terrorists to track down."

"It's a capsule that can track the white fleet."

Dark Reign grew silent and starkly serious. "What do you want for it?"

Alarms blared in the background, and Dark Reign's assistant rushed back into the room. "Sire, the fleet!" she yelled. "They have been spotted making guerilla attacks against our ships. They are coming out of zero space and annihilating us. Some reports even say they are coming back to finish off the homeworld." The sultan looked nervous, his eyes darting from side to side as fear showed on his face.

"How many and where?" Dark Reign asked.

She gave him a look of dismay as she handled a datapad. "It's chaos. Reports are coming in from all over. A complete panic. We have no idea what we are looking at. Seems to be thirty-two ships in eight different systems, with fourteen axes of attack."

"Send the information now," Dark Reign said to the sultan.

"Not so fast," the sultan replied. "I need to get rescued myself. Do you agree to my terms?"

"Yes. I'm sending a black ops team with cloaked entry. They will get you anywhere you need to go. Time is of the essence. We will negotiate the details later. If you don't send the information now, there will be no deal."

The sultan looked away and then back at the pressuring looks of Dark Reign and his assistant. The data pad in front of the assistant lit up. "The transmission is coming in," she said. "We have active tracking."

"Notify the fleet," said Dark Reign. "Everyone goes to zero space now."

# Chapter 18

Michael, the leader of the super black operations team, surveyed its members. His muscles bulged, and his look was intense, fierce, and a hundred percent serious. He didn't waver in his duty, his seriousness, or his command. He looked over his small but effective team. Five highly skilled men were all he needed to get any job done.

Kurt was the slimmest member of the team, but he was the technical genius. If they needed to override any system, he was the man. Michael looked Kurt over, inspecting the man for complete battle readiness. Kurt gave a knowing nod. His equipment and his tech were all ready to go.

Jax and Jay. They slammed chests, getting themselves psyched up. Then they rested their foreheads together. Their eyes were dead and staring straight-forward. They encompassed and embodied the brawn they brought to the table.

"I'm going to break their arms with my bare hands," said Jax.

"I'm going to knock them out with one punch," Jay replied.

Michael knew this wasn't an exaggeration. He'd seen both easily do so before. In fact, he would like to forget their numerous bar fights. Michael had needed to pull too many strings to keep them out of jail and still in the military.

Baruti looked calmly at the others while he fiddled with his explosives. He was hyper-confident and always very quiet. He was the demolitions expert of the group. Next to him stood the weirdo.

They called him Extra, although he preferred Midnight Extra. Every member of the group had very dark skin, more black than brown, but Extra was a special case. They used to call him the darkest soldier in the empire. Extra usually wore white face paint in an attempt to be ironic. It gave him a rather intimidating look. His clothes were too tight, and the colors were mismatched and with fluorescent accents. Extra clashed with the group like no other.

Michael stopped his physical inspection once he looked upon Extra. It was pointless. The man was an enigma to him, so why bother? Normally, Extra wouldn't be a member of the team, but he was deadly to no end, a weapons expert and sharpshooter. He was definitely the sniper that they needed.

"Who are we?" Michael shouted.

"Death's Witness!" his group responded.

"Who do we answer to?" Michael asked.

"Dark Reign himself!" the group shouted back.

"What do we do?" Michael asked.

"Witness the death of our enemies, sir!" the men exclaimed.

"Excellent. We are about to drop in on the sultan's party. The CDF has blockaded this planet, and they are bombing it from orbit. Will that stop us?"

"No, sir! We can infiltrate anywhere, sir!"

"Again."

"No, sir! We can infiltrate anywhere, sir!"

Michael smiled briefly. "I bet you are wondering why we took this giant ship. It's a little roomy for five people, isn't it?" His team smiled.

"I just thought you needed extra room to contain these guns." Jay pointed to his arms as his teammates laughed.

"Knock it off. We are going to rescue the sultan's whole bunker full of people," Michael said. The team members looked around, the expressions on their faces turning to dread as they realized the logistical nightmare they faced. "What's the matter? If this was easy, they would have called in the regulars. And if it was hard, they would have fucked it up. And if it was hard and they wanted it fucked up, they would have called black ops. But if it's impossible, and they want it done, who do they call?"

"Death's Witness!" the team shouted.

# Galactic Mandate: A Radical Cause

The spaceship descended undetected to the surface and landed two miles out from their target. The planet's desert climate was beating hard on their ship's engines, but Michael knew his ship could take it. After all, he was given only the best. *Even if something goes wrong, my team can handle it*, he thought.

They exited the ship, and an eerie quiet welcomed them to the foreign planet. Both Jax and Jay looked disappointed about the quiet welcome. "Do you think the CDF just ran away and gave up?" Jax asked.

"They better not. My arms ache. They haven't popped anyone's head in a while," Jay replied. Michael laughed. They all needed a chuckle to relieve the tension of having a casual stroll through enemy territory.

Kurt read his instrument. "A sizable force of enemies is around the bunker."

"Kurt, hack the satellites. I want to know what's in between us and the objective," Michael ordered.

"Yes, sir," Kurt replied.

A combat display showed holographic details of the battle situation. They all watched icons representing the rebels, the CDF soldiers, and what remained of the sultan's forces. Jax and Jay both smiled at the fact that twenty clone soldiers were headed directly toward their position, and they turned and ran directly towards the enemy. "Wait, it's a trap, you fools!" Michael shouted, but to no avail. Like bloodhounds that had gotten their first scent, there was no turning those two back. Michael came back to his senses. This was it. They didn't have time to plan. The enemy was coming to them whether they were prepared or not. *Why doesn't war just happen on my terms?* he joked to himself, and then he sprang into action.

"Kurt, get a line out to the sultan. I want them ready to extract to the ship on my signal. Extra, I need you to cover the main entrance to their bunker. Use your hive sniper kit. Baruti, bring the noise. You are going to create a distraction while you cut off reinforcements from using any routes that interfere with our plans. Remember, kiddos, we are here to get it done, not fuck it up like normies."

Each member of the team sprang to their duties, running through the battle-scarred streets. Extra shifted through the shadows, easily passing by the clones battling Jax and Jay. Michael watched him go and then provided assistance to the pair as they punched and brutalized the unprepared clones. He fired around his teammates, making sure no one took shots at them while they were busy in hand-to-hand combat. He could tell that they were enjoying themselves. *I'm going to have another talk with them when we get back. I'm not sure how many times I've told them to get serious,* he thought. Their arrogant street fighting worked. Soon, the twenty soldiers that had come to meet them were all lying on the ground, lifeless.

Michael and Kurt rushed to their position. "Kurt, what's the new tactical situation?" Michael asked.

"We cleared out the immediate threat," Kurt replied, "but there are still clashes around the bunker. Also, I don't know how we plan to get that many people out of here. Especially unnoticed."

"You leave that to me. I got a special surprise for y'all," Michael said.

Jax and Jay were pumped up; this was their first taste of battle in weeks. Michael watched as they smiled and yelled with excitement. "All right, time to cut that shit out!" he yelled.

Kurt took the hint and stepped in. "Let's go knock on the front door. The sultan is waiting," he said as he corralled the very amped Jax and Jay toward the entrance of the bunker.

"Oh boy, a brothel. I'm going to be on my best behavior for the ladies," Jay exclaimed sarcastically.

Michael unloaded a shoulder-fired blaster from his back. He pointed it back towards their spaceship and touched his heads-up display. It calculated distances and then methodically started to bring down parts of the buildings that were in the way. Loud bangs and pops, followed by crumbling, started to get the attention of both sides of the battle around them.

Baruti ducked and weaved through the battlefield, placing explosives at critical points, and sometimes, he was exposed to soldiers. "Sure you can cover him, Extra?" Michael asked.

"It's Midnight Extra to you, sir," said Extra.

"Whatever," Michael replied. He was still amazed at how well Extra could cover the team. He did the work of six snipers all linked together by his hive technology. Today, he wore a white helmet with small ports of mismatching colors that were linked to drone rifles that had flown themselves to different sniper nests around the bunker. Extra shot away at any soldiers that tried to get the drop on Baruti. Michael saw all of this as he continued to clear the space between the ship and the bunker.

"The sultan is ready to start the evacuation. We are waiting on your signal," Kurt relayed to Michael.

Michael continued to blast apart buildings, sometimes taking just three shots to crumble off a side. "Not yet. We won't get out of this so easily."

Kurt's tactical display lit up. "We got tanks incoming, along with more enemy troops. It looks like well-trained clones this time."

"That's what I was waiting for. They always like throwing some heavy metal at me," Michael said.

Baruti tapped his intercom. "I'm on it."

Jax, Jay, Kurt, and Michael started to come under fire. The tanks shelled their positions as they got to the brothel. This action, along with the rapid firing of lasers, bullets, and artillery was gathering the attention of more and more CDF soldiers. "If we don't turn down the heat fast, we will have the entire battle happening on our heads," Michael said.

Rebels started to appear from the rooftops of neighboring buildings. The air was dusty from the fragments of masonry, shrapnel, and other debris created by the fighting. Baruti continued to sneak around behind enemy lines as the tanks advanced. Midnight Extra was able to singlehandedly slow the advance of the clone troopers. His sniping made it seem like the team was firing from all directions. Dirt of various colors flew and settled around them, reds, yellows, and oranges glistening in the air.

"Extra," said Michael. "I mean Midnight Extra, or whatever you want to call yourself this week. I need you to make it seem as though the rebels are firing on the clones. This should split them up... Baruti, how is it coming on those tanks?"

"Just one more," Baruti replied. This was welcome news for Michael. He was holed up with the others behind various debris of the surrounding buildings and local abandoned vehicles.

The CDF fell for the deception Death's Witness portrayed. The soldiers were now not only firing on Michael's team but on the rebels as well. "Baruti, we can't wait any longer," Michael demanded. The tanks were making quick work of the rebel soldiers.

Just then, explosions erupted around the tank positions and around the city. "A job well done," Baruti called out because the heavy machinery was no longer a problem.

Extra turned his hive now on every enemy in sight, keeping most of the immediate battlefield distracted. Michael's team fired blasters, catching soldiers off guard, and they slaughtered those who took up arms against them. Clones were dying like the disposable henchman they were. "Get some!" Jax called out as they continued to dominate the battlefield.

"Looks like you were right, Major," said Kurt. "We are attracting a lot of attention. This is as slow as it's going to get. Reinforcements are landing everywhere from what I can see. We have about an hour until they are in range."

Michael tapped on the command console on his arm, accessing their ship's computer. "So, that surprise I had coming for you guys? Well, it's time to show you what it is. Go ahead and tell the sultan to come out. We just need to get out of the way."

Michael activated a cargo bay launch code. A giant, two-story shipping container launched from the ship, and it flew directly to their position. It was painted in a dull, urban camouflage pattern, and it had a large front opening with thick armor all around it. "Protect this container," Michael ordered, and the team took up defensive positions.

The sultan and his men rushed forward into the container. They filled up almost half of its entrance when the internal rotating platform lifted their level up, revealing another empty floor. The sultan, his elite guard, and Ninety-six watched as the other citizens from the bunker filled in the levels below them. This repeated until there was no one left to save.

Death's Witness continued to fight, holding off the encroaching enemy as their rescuees waited in their new shelter.

"That's a fancy rescue machine you got there," Jay said.

Midnight Extra interjected on the intercom: "Rescue machine? Really?"

"Shut up, fruit," Jax said, not wanting Extra to get a free laugh at his friend's expense.

"You call me a fruit when I don't think I've ever seen you guys around the ladies. Afraid to come out of the closet?" Extra replied.

Jax and Jay's faces grew red; a rage brewed within them.

"Settle down," said Michael. "Midnight's got a point. You guys need to stop holding each other's dicks and cover the extraction." He activated the storage container, and once more, the giant thrusters on its front flared up as it blasted itself back to the ship. Its rumbling clashed with the pitter-patter of bullets raining against its hull. "Time to activate our packs," Michael ordered.

They activated their jetpacks and followed the shipping container back to their ship, another job well done.

# Chapter 19

The fleet rushed into zero space. The various fleets of the empire scrambled to let loose a furious counterattack. With overwhelming force, battleships descended on the white fleet, annihilating it without mercy and consolidating the military around Dark Reign.

"The black ops team reported in. They secured the sultan and his entourage quickly and quietly. The CDF never knew they were there."

"Good. He will get governorship of a new backwater planet. Hmm. Looks like he made a deal at the right time."

# Chapter 20

Admiral Magnus Tareq was on high alert, sitting in the captain's chair. Tareq was the leader of the Conglomerate Republic's Clone Swarm Armada. He stared down the imperial advance as his forces waited. His lieutenants and captains begged for battle, but he knew better. The Conglomerate Republic had become a paper dragon with an atrophied, weak-willed citizenship backing them. They had no infrastructure to replace damaged ships, defense funding had been cut in half over the years, and the clone soldiers were worthless, ready to surrender at a moment's notice.

Calmer than ever before, Tareq looked over the tactical display. Intelligence officers had placed icons in the supposed locations where the leaders of imperial houses would be. They faced several fleets today, and not all the information was correct, but it could become important. He saw that God-Wrath and his imperial guard stood front and center. Scarlet Ember, the leader of House Scarlet, was to Reign's right, while the green fleet usually led by Mantis were to the left. The green fleet seemed to be acting unusually. *Maybe it was missing its leader.* The ships stood still in a blockade formation, waiting for more reinforcements from Dark Reign, military leader of the Imperial Armada. Tactically, it would be wise for Tareq to attack now, but this battle was not going to be won by force.

Dark Reign appeared out of zero space, his flagship, the *Nightmare*, surrounded by the remainder of the Imperial Armada. The command team looked at each other and at Tareq as all the ships started to appear on the screen. The entire Imperial Armada powered up their engines and moved toward the clone swarm. "Clear the command center," Tareq said. "Intelligence officers only."

The shocked crewmembers hurried out. Tareq could see the nervousness on their faces; if he didn't know what he was doing, their republic would fall today.

The admiral had made sure the swarm was fully battle-ready, so he was sure he had enough time to pull his stunt off. The intelligence officers cued a video in the background as they hailed the *Nightmare*. Dark Reign answered with only audio. "I suppose if you want to surrender to me directly, you can do that," he taunted.

"Trust me," the admiral replied, "when we are done here, you won't say that to me. I have a gift for you. Enable video, and I will show you the truth, if you can handle it. I will show you how your house of gods is a house of lies."

Dark Reign was intrigued. The video channel opened, and the intelligence officers of the clone swarm sprang into action. Soon, a video of the Drake research center was playing. When God-Reign's death came onscreen, the connection was immediately cut off by Dark Reign. An older intelligence officer said to Tareq, "We hacked the armada's communications network. They all saw that."

Admiral Tareq smiled. The day was won.

The armada stopped advancing towards them. Though they had already passed into Republic territory, Admiral Tareq held his forces from firing on the imperials. *Territory is never an exact science*, he thought. Then he sat back in his seat and watched his plan play out.

Dark Reign started firing on the Imperial Guard.

\*\*\*

God-Wrath panicked as everything started crumbling around him. It took only a second for him to control his senses so that he could think of a way out of this. A civil war had started on the day that was supposed to be his greatest victory.

Mantis and House Green stayed loyal to Dark Reign, but Wrath still had his considerable Imperial Guard. Some loyalist had taken over some random ships, but it was not enough to swing the battle to his favor.

Scarlet Ember's ship exploded from another blow, and he watched as his mother-in-law died. This sent the forces of House Scarlet retreating from the battle, as they no longer had any stake in the matter. Scarlet Lilly screamed in agony in the background, wailing for her mother. As his only ally was in full retreat, Commander Skyfall looked to God-Wrath for guidance.

"Send a distress call," he commanded.

\*\*\*

Admiral Tareq enjoyed the show, as everything was going as planned. "Sir, distress calls are going out. Do you want to jam them?" an officer asked.

"No, let this play out," Tareq commanded.

Suddenly, a mercenary fleet appeared. These ships provided limited cover as God-Wrath's flagship, the *God's Hand*, retreated. It was only enough to give the ship some time, not enough to save it from its impending doom.

Dark Reign's forces exited in the opposite direction, leaving God-Wrath's forces at the mercy of the CDF.

\*\*\*

Skyfall looked at God-Wrath again as the ship sparked and exploded around them. His eyes met hers as he ran. She tried to interrupt him as he exited. "Wait!" she called out. He didn't stop. Running to an escape pod, he left Skyfall to the ruined ship.

\*\*\*

Admiral Tareq left the command center and went to his quarters, where two guards were waiting. "Your new arrivals came," one informed as he walked past. Tareq entered his bedroom and looked around. Two cloned women stood at the back of the room, designed to be exactly the same except for skin tone. He took the one to his liking and threw her on the bed. She cringed but did not make a noise, as she was trained not to; the guard had informed her of what had happened to the last clones. Tareq gave her a demanding look, as he had just completed a job well done and wanted his prize. This was what his considerable salary paid for, and he would not be denied this night.

The other clone cowered back against the wall. She tried to leave.

"No, you watch. You are going to learn or be recycled," he threatened.

The clone on the bed stared at Tareq as he undressed. He kept moving closer and closer to her, and she could not escape what was about to happen. Soon, this clone's mind would retreat to a happier place. Soon, she would block out her surroundings as she wondered if the rumors were true: *Is there an armada coming to free me?*

# Chapter 21

Two months later

The *Vessel* shone in the sun as it orbited the planet and began its approach. The gold vessel with black trim looked as regal as ever, as God-Wrath piloted towards the planet Dominion, steering gently, awaiting the inevitable communication from below. Soon, planetary control would call, asking for identification, customs, and clearance. Not waving any of the passport information, he pondered how to get in illegally. There had been numerous videos played before him at the royal palace on Emortono on how to stop such activity; now he called upon that knowledge to get him planetside.

"Unidentified vessel, state your business here," a customs officer said.

"Just visiting some old friends."

"Tell me which city, and we will get you assigned to a spaceport."

God-Wrath's thoughts darted back and forth; he was unsure of what to say next. The names of the cities flew through his head, but then, as if on cue, he remembered where he might find a sympathetic ally to help him regain his throne, or at least stay hidden for a while. "Old Bane City," he replied confidently.

"All right," the customs officer replied. "Head on down. The spaceport is big. You can't miss it."

Afterburners flared as he descended down to the coordinates transmitted by the customs officer. Turning on the autopilot, he got himself ready to appear in front of others. It had been a long journey, and he hadn't stopped to take a break in a while. *When you lose an empire, you don't look your best*, he thought.

The subtle nudge of landing and real gravity informed him that he had arrived. Brewmaster Spaceport was the largest port on Dominion, and it was in the heart of Old Bane City. It had been nicknamed Smugglemaster by the locals, but that wasn't its official title. The sun burned him as he left the shelter of his ship. A customs officer confronted him right away. The big military man looked him in the eyes.

A bit threatened since he didn't have the height advantage, God-Wrath's hand hovered above his blaster, ready for any trouble. "Look, I need to get on this planet quietly and discreetly. I've heard it's not too much of a problem around this neck of the galaxy." God-Wrath knew his forwardness would be off-putting, but he had no choice.

The customs officer looked around, making sure no one was in earshot. He had recognized his imperial highness right away, and he knew God-Wrath was on the imperial wanted list, but that didn't matter much to him. Most of his customers were known criminals. The horrible ones and terrorists he would arrest on sight. The officer didn't hold any ill will against the empire, and his administrator's job paid pretty well, especially when you counted the untaxed tips he received. Deciding to play along, he asked. "How much you got for me?"

God-Wrath reached for his pocket computer and rested it on his arm. He started to look through his accounts. Much to his surprise, all of his funds were frozen. The computer beeped in error, informing not only God-Wrath of the problem, but the guard as well. The guard looked disappointed, as any hope of a giant payday was gone. Looking up at the ship, the customs officer realized it was worth quite a fortune. A new imperial escape vessel and one that had allowed God-Wrath to escape—the customs officer started to think about time and how, in a few years, this vessel could really make him some cash at auction. That wouldn't happen if he made an arrest.

# Galactic Mandate: A Radical Cause

"Well. It looks like you are new at this, so I'm going to do you a solid. I'll take your ship there, and you can go on your way. Although you might want to change."

God-Wrath agreed. He went back onto the *Vessel* and put on some more common clothes. After a quick shave, he was ready, and he made his way into the city. A little bit frightened of being all alone in a strange city by himself, he got out his mobile devices, turned off any tracking, and immediately tried to find any contacts in the area, but he came up short. No family members were around; they wouldn't frequent a planet like this. As he moved through the crowds, he tried to seem busy, like he was going somewhere. He was going nowhere, but he couldn't stand out. He kept his eyes alert to his surroundings, watching out for any guards or imperials who might try to turn him in. His stomach was starting to growl; he hadn't eaten anything in a while.

Two missionaries spotted him and struck up a conversation. God-Wrath's instincts were to run, but acting irrationally would only arouse suspicion at this point. "You look worn out and hungry. First time on Dominion?" one of the missionaries, a young man, asked. He and his companion, a woman, offered God-Wrath food, and he accepted. They explained that they ran a mission not too far from the spaceport, and they offered him room and board. God-Wrath sucked up his pride and accepted. He didn't want to, but right now, he had no choice. It had been a long day, and he needed to get used to the planet's time and the normal schedule.

That night, he stayed in a bunk bed with three strangers around him. Their names escaped him, and he didn't seem to fit in. The strangers were just looking to spend a warm night in a shelter and move on in the morning to look for work. Whether that was more seedy or honest, he couldn't tell. Like him, they took the generosity of the missionaries for granted and moved on.

In the morning, God-Wrath started to look for his political contacts. He had to decide between Lord Hate and his underground rival, Vlad Bane, the baron's little brother. Feeling that Lord Hate would be monitored due to their recent transactions and dealings via Skyfall, he decided to reach out to the latter. He didn't have much to offer Lord Hate at this point, but Vlad could easily be manipulated. He could offer to help remove Lord Hate when he regained power. Also, Vlad had family in the capital who had survived the bombing. Even without his imperial power in the capital, he could still hold some sway behind closed doors. Getting in touch with Vlad's people was easy: a few phone calls and a couple of names dropped, and they answered. Finding them, on the other hand, was hard. Their location was not public record. They arranged for a hover car to pick him up. He had to walk to the main square of the city, and they flew him in from there.

The hovercar landed at a midsized house on top of a hill overlooking the city. The place reminded him of Brian Bane's prison complex, but it was a lot smaller and a lot less fortified. This was just a house with a lot of war supplies scattered about. The rebels met him and led him into the house, to a makeshift command center converted out of the living room. Vlad stood with his rebel brothers and soldiers. There were five of them in total, plus the two guards who stood behind God-Wrath.

"God-Wrath," said Vlad, "how nice to finally meet you in person. You said that you needed something from me?"

"Yes, I need a ship and crew. You give me that, and I will give you legitimacy when I retake the throne," God-Wrath offered, waving his hand in a regal manner.

"You can't offer shit. In fact, why don't I just kill you know? Save the empire some trouble?"

"Because I happen to know that you sent your wife and kids to live on Gothica, a nice, safe world where no one can get to them. So you thought. I also happen to know Snapdragon. Have you heard of her?"

Vlad's eyes grew worried. Everyone in the room grew uneasy, as they had all heard this name before and thoughts of the scarlet assassin ran through their heads. The memory from news reports of how dangerous this woman was put a little bit of fear into their hearts. She was a woman they didn't want to mess with. Vlad moved around the table. Slowly and with authority, he brought his face close to God-Wrath's. "You better be able to back this up."

"I want my crew. I want funds. You owe it to your emperor."

The tension was thick. The guards slowly surrounded God-Wrath as Vlad moved his hand to his laser cannon. God-Wrath, defenseless, stared directly into Vlad's eyes, ignoring the others, preparing to choke him with his bare hands if he had to. Mentally, he pictured how to cause as much harm as physically possible before his demise.

A sudden whistle disrupted the silence. Soon, it was a blaring alarm in the background. Not moving from their positions, everyone looked around. They were a little dazed and extremely confused. The two guards rushed to the windows, and their eyes widened at the sight of two large battering rams coming at the house at full speed. They could clearly see the special operations police, in full black garb, riding on the sides of the flying vehicles. Frightened and unprepared for a siege, they turned and shouted, "Run! They found us!"

Breaking from their confrontation, everyone turned and scattered. Seconds later, the doors caved in. The long, rectangular battering ram punched through, and then it was released by the police APV, falling flat on Vlad and crushing him instantly. His blood leaked out underneath this new walking platform.

The rebels were still running, trying to escape their fate. The special operations soldiers started to pour into the dwelling, fanning out to identify potential threats and securing the initial breach for the arrival of Dark Braylon and Dark Cleo, brother and sister, the children of Dark Reign. Dark Braylon was just sixteen years old, and his sister was a more mature twenty-four.

Braylon was young and foolish, rushing in with no patience, as he could not wait to lead the charge. Using his laser cannon, he shot two guards as they tried to escape, not waiting for their surrender. "Enough!" barked Cleo. "We must capture these rebels. We don't want to kill God-Wrath by accident and not finish the mission." She had rainbow colors in her natural black hair, all of which fell to the right side, as she had shaved the left of her scalp. She was a skinny woman, but her body was all toned muscle. She was a lot stronger than most women her size.

She carried a netting gun, and she gave one to her brother. They rushed down the halls, checking rooms and eventually making their way outside, where God-Wrath and the last two remaining guards had been caught rushing to put on jetpacks. God-Wrath frantically strapped himself into his pack, not stopping even to look at the special ops team running up to him. The rebels and God-Wrath finished putting on the jetpacks before the police could reach them, and then each blasted off in a different direction.

Something stopped God-Wrath's progress, and he looked down and saw that the teenage boy had shot and secured a rope around his leg. The netting sparked and threw out flames as it slowed, stopped, and then began pulling God-Wrath in. He could see the rebels around him getting roped in as well. The others were not so lucky, the torque from being caught sending them full speed into the ground, killing them instantly.

God-Wrath frantically started firing at the ground so the same fate would not befall him. He had a kinetic bolt blaster, the only weapon he had been able to find in his hectic escape. One shot left a hole in the chest of Braylon. The child let go, but so did the jetpack, and God-Wrath found himself on the ground, surrounded by police, while Braylon's sister screamed, crying over the loss of her little brother.

# Chapter 22

Danica, Kai, and Mantis shared a prison cell in the dungeon. Mantis banged his fist against the hard iron bars keeping them in. "Give me my armor. You'll regret it. Come on, Blooden aren't so tough—"

His ranting was interrupted by Danica giving him a punch to the back of the head. "Looks like you're not a tough guy anymore, *Lord*," she said sternly. Mantis turned and threw a few punches at her, but they were soft due to the atrophy of his arms. Shocked at how powerless Mantis was without his armor, Danica took the blows.

"Watch it. You almost broke my breathing tube," Mantis said.

"I'm going to break something, all right." She landed a swift kick to his crotch, sending an expression of intense pain across his face.

"Stop assaulting a superior," Kai ordered.

"He is no superior," she replied, still beating on Mantis.

"I'll need you to keep your strength so you can get us out of here," said Kai.

Laughter erupted from a woman in the cell across from them. "Going to bust out of here and show them what's what, are you?" the voluptuous woman asked. Her native tattoos covered her reddish, sun-kissed skin. One long braid flowed from the top of her head to the middle of her back, and her brown eyes were filled with sarcasm. She was wearing only a ragged brown tube top, all that remained of a once full blouse, and a just-as-ragged skirt made from the same material. "Let me show you the only thing you're about to do in here." She dropped her top and ripped off her shirt, exposing herself to the newcomers. Her top had been holding back more than enough breast. Her breasts were perky, and they looked as hard as rock. Her skin rippled around the edges. This tribal woman bent down, staring at everyone across from her. She wanted them to see her.

Two of the men in her cell did not react. The third man stomped his way forward, his muscles bulging, fully clothed except for a raging erection. He was shorter than expected for a man of his bulk, four hundred pounds, and he shook the ground when he walked. His large arms were offset by below-average legs. He was obviously an islander from the tone of his skin and the radically unique tattoos. He penetrated the willing woman in front of their eyes with no shame or embarrassment.

"I'm CJ, and this is Boulder." Her breathing shortened as she started to enjoy the rough sex that she was presenting to them. Her words started to come quicker and with less breath behind them. "If you try to leave, you'll be as fucked as I am."

Nervously, Kai, Danica, and Mantis looked away as the initial shock started to wear off. "Don't you look away," the woman commanded. "You need to see this." She started to push back on the man, rocking and matching his rhythm and his speed. Abruptly, she stopped. "That's enough, Boulder." The man's smile dropped, and he faded back into the shadows of their shared prison cell.

"Still trying your best to outdo a man?" Mantis asked. He was still heaving from one of Danica's punches to the chest. Kai no longer asked or cared about old ranks. *I'll report everything to my superiors and let them deal with it*, he thought. *Besides, an Acolyte lord should be able to fend for himself.* The fact that Mantis needed his help at all had Kai questioning the man's authority. *Why am I reporting to someone so weak in the face of a little imprisonment?*

"Time for a refill!" one of the prison guards yelled. Kai and Danica rushed to the cell door, and they stuck their compressed liquid oxygen canisters in between the bars. The oxygen would last for about a month before requiring a refill. The guards provided more, popping the old ones out and exposing the prisoners to the poison air, which used to affect them immediately. Now they could last the entire changeover without noticing. Mantis hobbled over, making it just in time before the guards moved on. He was more cautious than his friends, holding his breath for the entire changeover. The guards looked at Kai and the others and then gave them a hand gesture of disrespect. Then they left with smiles on their faces, moving down the hall and out of the cell block.

Kai turned to Danica and then looked around for CJ, making sure she was not listening. "Here's the plan," he said rather loudly. "I have a bunch of tools hidden behind that stone we loosened up over the months we've been here. I'm just waiting on the guard to come with the keys tomorrow, and then we can escape." He shot Danica a wink. She looked confused, but she decided to play along.

"What do you need me to do?" she asked.

"I need you to create a disturbance tomorrow when they come by for dinner. Then we can make our move."

"What tools do you have?"

"A lockpick and a communicator."

"How did you get them? I've been with you every second," she asked, obviously confused.

Kai gave her a very serious stare in response. He moved his mouth but did not speak, gesturing that the conversation was over. He could see CJ watching over Danica's shoulder, and her attention was piqued. Kai couldn't tell how much she had heard.

"What kind of distraction are we talking about here?" Mantis asked. His interest was also piqued.

"I was thinking she could give you another one of those beatings," Kai replied.

"Not funny. When I get out of here, I'll have you both hanged," said Mantis.

Danica laughed and raised her fist in another bit of anger. Kai put his hand over it, lowering the tension in the room. "In all seriousness, let's figure that out. I don't think we will get more than one shot."

"Let's have the woman yell. That's all she's good for," said Mantis.

"You are not helping," Danica replied. "If you don't have anything useful to say, just sit in your corner and let the adults handle this."

"I was thinking of something a little more useful," said Kai. "Something simple. Just having you throw food at the guards. That should bring them in for a quick tussle."

They all agreed and then went back to their usual activity of sitting and waiting. Kai recounted things from his training. Danica told stories of her family. Mantis told everyone their fates once he escaped, which, according to him, they all should fear.

Soon, the guards rushed in. Batons in hand, they made sure to put their weight into every swing. Kai and his group covered their heads as they cowered back into their corners. "Where is it? Where is the contraband?" the lead guard demanded. He was pudgy, and he stood in a strong, towering stance.

The sounds of the crowded room overwhelmed Kai. Danica looked defiant while shielding her face, a contradiction that infuriated the guards. They had to hold themselves back as the rage boiled within them. Mantis, already meeker in form and stature, got prodded with their shock batons.

"We received a tip that there is contraband in the cell and that you are trying to escape. Well, that's not going to happen on my watch. No one has ever escaped!" the guard shouted at the prisoners.

Kai held back a smile. "All right, I'll tell. Just stop beating me."

The guard stopped. CJ and her cohorts assembled by the cell doors, watching the scene unfold. The other prisoners started to stomp and make a ruckus. "Quiet down, or your cells are next!" the leader yelled, but to no avail. The entire prison erupted in contradicting yells of support, condemnation, and just incomprehensible chatter. The prisoners yelled random sayings and anything they could think of.

"It's behind the panel over here," said Kai.

The guards removed the panel and looked within. "There is nothing there," said the lead guard. "Let's get out of here. The prisoners are just trying to get some entertainment out of us, apparently."

The panel was, in fact, empty. *Just the way I left it*, Kai thought. More panels were loose, and the guards were the target. Kai and Danica moved with swiftness, smacking the guards down and then overwhelming them and seizing their batons. Background noise helped mask their sudden escape, and they ran through the open door.

Kai stopped to give a quick thank you to someone essential to his plan. "Thanks, CJ. We couldn't have done it without you."

Mantis slowly followed the others out the door as prisoners screamed taunts and threatened sexual and physical punishments.

The three came to a command center. The guard looked at them with surprise, his tan uniform blending in with the computers. A quick shock from a baton subdued him, but not before he could hit the alarm. Danica hit him with some unnecessary blows to make sure he didn't get up soon. "What's the rest of this plan?" she asked.

"I don't have one," Kai replied.

"I think I can help you there," said Mantis. "We won't escape. There is no way without my armor and with a woman slowing us down. But this central control should have a galactic radio. We can call Dark Reign to give him the code, 'falling green'. He'll take care of the rest."

"We're not listening to you," Danica replied.

"Really? Tell me, what was your grand scheme? All we've done is piss off the guards, and there is no way out of here. You need my codes. The ones you have won't even cause the imperial janitors to panic."

Kai raised his eyebrows, dropped the tension in his mouth, and relaxed for a second. "He has a point," he said.

"If we're going to do this," said Mantis, "we have to do it now. We don't have any more time to use my codes if you want to get out of here."

Kai picked up the galactic radio and said the words. Then they turned to the door as though they expected it to be immediately blasted open by a rescue party. They had fantasies of leaving the prison right away. Nothing greeted them but silence.

A burst of static came over the radio.

"Is that our people?" Danica asked. Mantis shrugged, giving them the impression that he didn't know any more than they did.

They could hear the guards running down the hall to the command center. Kai reached for the button to close the door, shutting them off from the rest of the prison.

"Grab your weapons. We have to fight our way out," Danica said.

Kai gripped his baton, ready to give some well-deserved revenge to the prison guards.

"Open up! You're going to regret this!" the lead guard yelled over the alarm and through the door.

*How are we going to get out of this?* Kai thought.

The doors raised up at the same time, and the alarm shut off. The lead guard smiled as he walked into the room. Kai and the others were surrounded, all entrances and exits covered by new guards that had been called in to assist. Shocks interrupted their surprise, and then everything went black.

***

Kai awoke back in a cell with Danica and Mantis. It had been a couple of days since their breakout attempt. CJ taunted from across the hall, her large hands gripping the cell door while she yelled at them, telling them how this was still her prison.

"Will you shut up?" Kai yelled.

"No. It's you who needs to be a quiet prisoner." The lead guard was back this time with a larger entourage.

"Told you I run this bitch," CJ taunted.

Danica looked at Kai, who appeared to be looking for an answer he couldn't give. Mantis waited in the background, bored but glad that the hostility between him and his cellmates had ceased for the time being.

"Because of the stunt you pulled a couple of days ago," the guard said, "I'm having you all transferred."

CJ laughed. "Told you it's my prison. Get out. You cause too much trouble anyway."

"Not so fast," said the guard. "You are going with them. You gave us bad information. You were in on it."

"I wasn't! I swear!" CJ replied.

"Well, too bad. I don't want your loud mouth around here anymore anyway. You all are going to have so much fun at the Shore. I bet it will be a vacation." The guards all laughed at once.

"You can't do this. My tribe will get revenge. They will get revenge," CJ complained.

"Shut up, or you won't make it even to the Shore," the guards said. Turning his attention back to Kai's group, he handcuffed and shackled the prisoners.

Kai didn't resist. He had no more plans to escape. *I shouldn't have listened to Mantis. What does that cripple know, anyway? How could he have fallen so low?*

Danica still resisted, pushing where she could. The guards struggled to get her in the right direction, but they couldn't let off the impression that one of the prisoners was too much for them to handle. They grabbed CJ next, handcuffing her and then pushing her down the hall. Boulder came rushing to her defense, but he was met with baton after baton of shocks. "Boulder!" CJ cried. "I love you." Boulder just grunted as shocks surged through his body.

Mantis got up to put his hands behind his back, waiting to be handcuffed and shackled like the rest. "Nope, you don't get to go with the others. She's got special plans for you," the lead guard stated.

"What's that?" Mantis asked as the guards closed the door. They also closed Boulder's cell, leaving him to his smaller roommates. They sat with their heads down, broken from what they had seen and endured. With all the cells locked again, the guards left.

Mantis could hear the slow clicking of heels from the other side of the hall. He walked up to the bars and looked out, his eyes trying to adjust to the different lighting, but to no avail. He couldn't see anything but a small silhouette that matched the clicking pace as it drew near. Slowly, the figure grew, and the pace increased. The clicking grew into a chorus of clanks: the familiar sound of the jackboots of enforcers. He had loved that sound when they had worked for him.

The Blood Queen emerged with her entourage of elite Blooden guards. These looked rougher than before. They showed more exposed skin with more tattoos, which made a menacing display meant to terrify their enemies. "If it isn't my new husband," she laughed. "My, my, these accommodations don't suit you. Get him out of here."

They took the handcuffed man and pushed him down the hallway, away from his friends. They shoved him along to keep pace with the Blood Queen, but otherwise, they made sure to keep their distance. He couldn't get too close without the guards becoming alert and agitated.

# *Chapter 23*

Kai sat in the prisoner transport shuttle with Danica and a very upset CJ, who cried and wiggled around in the cold gray transport. She tried to break free from her chains and punish Kai and Danica with her bare hands, but she couldn't. They all sat in the back of the shuttle, cut off from the prison guards like cargo as it flew through the air. They could see small clouds in a dingy, polluted sky through some small, reinforced windows, but nothing else.

"I wonder what the Shore will be like. Has to be better than that stupid prison," Danica said.

"It doesn't sound so bad," Kai replied.

CJ shook her head in disbelief. "You idiots just gave us a death sentence," she said.

"What do you know?" Kai asked.

CJ shrugged.

"I would answer the question if I were you," said Danica. "Don't want the guards to learn how everything was your plan. I'm sure they can cook up something worse than the Shore for you."

"But that's not true," said CJ.

"They don't know that," Danica replied.

"The Shore is a small ocean prison surrounded by water. They put you in cages year-round and laugh at you while they wait for you to die. And if you try to escape, the guns mounted on the surrounding rock shoot you until you are fish meat."

"That doesn't sound too much worse than where we were at," Kai rebutted.

"Simpleton. I hope they leave your cage open," said CJ, directing an angry look at them.

"At least you won't be the prison queen, or whatever you thought you were," Danica said with a laugh.

The shuttle flew by the prison as it spiraled down to an airfield. Kai and Danica stood up as far as they could to get a better look, though they were still halfway crouched due to the restraints. They could see the whitewater waves crashing against the cages. The orange and brown rock created a natural perimeter wall around the prison. The cages were barely above the ocean's surface. They were few in number, and the prison wasn't that large, just the airstrip, a small structure, and the cages. They saw some sun-struck prisoners lying down, floating whenever a wave hit.

Soon, the shuttle landed, and then Kai, Danica, and CJ were herded to a cage. "Hope you enjoy the next couple of months," one of the guards said, and they laughed as they left. The cold water greeted the three prisoners as a warm sun beat down. The air was soggy, and it smelled of damp, moldy, unwashed clothes. Garbage lined the bottom of the cages, flowing in and out with the waves.

"What does he mean, 'next couple of months'?" Danica asked.

"The tide eventually drowns everyone here. This prison is underwater in the summer. I promised myself I wouldn't die like my dad, but here I am, in the same prison and about to die the same way." CJ returned to crying.

"Not us. We have our oxygen filters," Kai said.

"They won't refill them anymore," said Danica. "This is a slow execution." She watched Kai's expression as he lost all hope. Then she offered a quick solution to ease her fallen commander. "I think I can make the filters work with water to extend their life, but it won't work forever. We might get an extra month tops before they give out under the extra strain."

Kai looked only slightly relieved. "I don't know what to do," he said.

# Chapter 24

"Traitor is being transported to his execution."

"It can't come soon enough."

"Can you believe his family wanted us to worship this prick?"

"I'm glad the military took over."

"No more of this tribal BS. We will get a real leader with strength."

"Yeah, someone who knows which fights they can and can't win."

The room was dark, and God-Wrath was blindfolded. He could hear the guards talking—a dull conversation about issues they knew very little about, if anything at all. He couldn't move his arms or legs. All he could do was sit and listen to the continued bragging by the guards. The spaceship they were on moved like it was experiencing turbulence; the artificial gravity was not as stable as it was on the large ships he was used to.

"Yes, this should be a nice and easy drop."

"Aren't they all?"

"Oh, man, you are young."

"How so?"

"Well, anything can happen, especially out here. These remote space regions can be hell sometimes. On our first run, we ran into an actual space gang. They tried to break out their leader. Some thug zealot they recognized as their gangster messiah."

"What happened?"

"Well, we had some surprise for them. The rinky-dink ship they tried to use didn't last long. Come to think of it, maybe he was their messiah, because they're all in a better place now."

"Hahaha."

"Haha."

"Those were the days, kid. Those were the days."

"I bet this ship was new back then."

"Shut up."

Alarms started blaring. The radio communicators on the guards' uniforms activated in unison. "There are dead bodies," someone said over the radio. "What the fuck happened here? Oh, my God, they aren't dead."

"Control, what? You're not making sense. Dead bodies in space?"

"Don't worry about it. Just protect the package."

"They are coming through on all decks," another voice said over the radio.

God-Wrath couldn't hear anything but the alarm for several seconds. Then he heard grunting and shuffling as the guards got into battle-ready stances. "Dispatch, what happened to the bodies?"

The guards waited for several seconds, but there was no response.

"What happened to them?"

"The same thing that will happen to us if we don't defend this."

"Ahhh!"

Blaster, flashbangs, counterfire. God-Wrath tried to make sense of it all. But nothing came to mind but confusion. He could make out sounds but not with any context.

Then the blackness lifted. "God-Wrath. We have found a good prize today. Are you ready to keep the light?"

The head Keeper was standing in front of God-Wrath, looking out the window at his home: the asteroid shipyards, where giant vertical halos picked asteroids out from the field and mined them for raw materials. Built on the outer rings of a black hole, the system was devoid of natural light. The Keepers' skin reflected this. Though still of a dark pigment due to the way the light system worked on the halo, their skin had a washed-out look to it. The pigment wasn't uniform but was patchy, with lighter and dark spots. They said the Keepers could tell which halo you were from and who your parents were from how your spots looked.

"We are going to have lots of fun with you, God-Wrath. I can think of so much you will learn." The Keeper smiled.

"What are you going to do with me?" God-Wrath asked.

"That's the fun part. We call it aggressive re-education."

\*\*\*

Three months later

God-Wrath wondered what new toy of torture they were going to use on him today. What would they think of? He stood chained to the wall of the cell. He hoped it wasn't the water cage. This was a large box filled with a unique gel that could be electronically controlled to simulate drowning one moment and then allow the person to breathe perfectly fine the next. He hated how it could switch so quickly and sporadically. This torture was horrible, but so were others. Just like this new torture he was about to discover.

"We've got something new for you," the head Keeper said. "It's going to teach you the consequences of your actions." He looked at God-Wrath with great joy. In his hand was a new electro lash.

God-Wrath knew this was bad. *They have two doctors this time*, he thought. *This is going to be horrible.* "Stop! I can't take it! I don't even know what you want," he yelled.

The whipping had already started. He screamed out in agony.

"The lashes represent five hundred people who died since the civil war started," said the head Keeper. "Trust me, we will be here for a while."

"Why, why are you doing this?" God-Wrath asked.

The head Keeper smiled but refused to answer. "The doctor to our left, well, his job is to keep you awake and alert. So, no napping for you. And you see the one on the right? Her job is to heal your back so we can keep going until we are done." The Keeper smiled again at the reaction in God-Wrath's eyes. "Yes, this is the reaction I was waiting for. You are ready soon. I have a guest, and she has been waiting for you to be ready."

The Keeper savored the confusion in God-Wrath's eyes. God-Wrath did not know he could communicate so much with his eyes, as the Keeper almost seemed to be reading his mind. At least if he kept him talking, the whipping slowed down to a bearable pace. This time, he decided to ask his question again. "I need to know why they are doing this to me. The is no reason to just torture without end. This isn't the way of the Acolytes. Tell me why!"

"Because the cause deserves a better leader," the head Keeper stated.

\*\*\*

Three months later

God-Wrath stood amongst warriors. After the lashing, he had learned to fight with them every day. At first, it had been cruel, one-sided beatings and punishment. Then he had learned to resist and then to fight back. Over time, God-Wrath's skills had grown until they were comparable to the warriors'.

The new Keepers, with their patchwork skin, surrounded him. *Just as I planned*, he thought. Three of the warriors rushed forward in a lazy attempt to overwhelm him. A quick elbow to both stopped their advances. The third hit him in the kidney repeatedly. This caused a rush of pain, but it was nothing too unexpected. God-Wrath countered swiftly, breaking the glee of the attacker.

The others stepped back as the head Keeper emerged from the background. "Looks like you are finally ready," he said in his irritatingly gross voice.

Another figure came out of the background. This time, God-Wrath felt his heart surge when he recognized the person. His most trusted commander. "Skyfall, you betrayed me with this torture." She seemed to lack the emotional depth that he remembered, and she looked battle-worn.

# Galactic Mandate: A Radical Cause

She replied, "I, we, have made you better, someone worthy of leading us. The cause deserved it."

The head Keeper butted in. "I have a gift for you. It will make everything better."

A giant window blast shield started to open, revealing a new fleet of ships, white and with the God-Wrath logo in the center of their cylindrical bodies. He could see two large clusters of ships, with a very large capital ship in the center, larger than he had ever seen.

"We now have the tools to complete the cause," said the head Keeper.

Skyfall approached God-Wrath and intimately embraced his arm. "Let me catch you up on what you have missed."

# Chapter 25

Darnell Treycove, the planetary governor, looked out the window as they passed the crystal dams. It sparkled with refracted colors as it held back crystal blue waters. It was another long day of refugee camp visits. This time, it was Camp Goober, set up for the clones by God-Wrath. The governor's shuttle flew through the air, closely following a river. They flew past greenhouse pyramids that were about five stories tall. They were filled with life and had irrigation flowing between them. These were surrounded by a normal-looking large city. They flew past skyscrapers and apartment buildings until they finally found a recycling dump. It served as a holding ground for garbage before it was recycled later. Then he saw it: the white tents and the many similar faces. It was the camp. He remembered a time when these visits had been unnecessary.

A subtle descent to the camp, and Darnell was in action. He greeted children, met with families, and took pictures of happy clones living their lives. He also avoided any questions about the future. *Is there ever going to be a permanent place for them?* He couldn't give those answers, especially not now. "Where is the Goddess?" he asked his security detail, feeling lost. The camp had that effect on people because its tents all looked the same. The people looked the same, the children, and the stray junk lying around. There was not much one could do to gain a sense of direction.

"I think she is coming to us." Darnell's question was answered by a million different rays of the sun being redirected and causing a brief blindness in him. His guards lowered their sunglasses and bowed in respect. Goddess

# Galactic Mandate: A Radical Cause

Medica walked slowly in her long, golden dress, followed by her golden maiden and guards. They passed out food and water to the clone refugees. Her hair was long and white with golden-dyed tips to match her outfit. Her skin was a slightly dark brown that seemed to glow along with her outfit. "Imani, it's so good to see you, my dear," Darnell said, bravely welcoming Goddess Medica with her old name, the one he knew her by. She smiled, which looked as out of place as she did among the trash dump. "Have you heard your son is on his way?" Darnell continued.

"Yes, it will be lovely to see him again. I hope he can help with giving supplies to the clones. He always loved to do that," she replied.

"I don't think it's going to be that simple. In fact, you need to come with us. It's not safe here." Darnell gave a nod to his security guards, who surrounded the Goddess and her guards.

"Stop all this nonsense. My son would never harm me or these clones," Medica said. Her golden warriors flanked Darnell's guards. They didn't outnumber the guards, but they outgunned them with white and gold blaster rifles. They almost raised them aggressively, but they knew to let the politicians fight it out verbally.

"I'm sure he wouldn't, but it's not just him. You heard what happened last week. We can't let you just stay in the middle of a refugee camp any longer. I'm responsible for your protection, and I can't lose any more of our citizens."

A horn sounded in the background. The air-raid sirens blared suddenly but expectedly. The clones scrambled, searching for shelter in their tents, moving junk and supplies to create forts of hard plastic to protect them from what was coming. Darnell looked up at the Emortono sky and spied specks of light that shouldn't have been there. Emergency services started to respond by sending shuttles and spaceships flying everywhere.

"Sir," said one of Darnell's guards, "we have planetary control on the line. We still need to get you back to the bunker with or without the Goddess."

Debris started to fall down to the surface, hitting the building, starting fires, and creating explosions. The gentle day had turned chaotic. "You better get going, Darnell," said Medica. "My fate is tied to these people. If they die, I'm going with them. And that is an order from your Goddess." Her golden guard stood down. They knew it was over, as Darnell was rushed back into the shuttle by his guards. "Devante, what mess are you starting today?" Medica asked as she looked up at the oncoming debris. A gathering of maidens and children circled around her as she headed back to her tent. They sang and hummed, and some even outright prayed to her for her help. She walked, dragging the train of her dress back to her golden camp. "Do not worry. The mighty Acolyte Empire will protect you."

Darnell could no longer see Medica; she was completely surrounded by the clone refugees. He contacted planetary control from a table-sized computer inside his shuttle. "Mandatory overtime for all emergency personnel," he ordered over video chat. "Get the response crews up in the sky. We will be helping everyone who comes falling from the sky. Take no sides. We can't afford to. We are still cleaning up after the last attack, so no one gets any sleep until this one is over." The young man on the other end saluted and ended the video call. The screen changed from the chat to smaller video feeds of emergency crews responding to the various fires and ships descending from the sky, damaged beyond repair.

The shuttle lifted off and sped to a newly created bunker for government officials. It had been hastily built and was still unfinished, but he didn't want to take any chances. Anyone who was important was headed that way. Air traffic was limited right now to only emergency vehicles and the random space pilots who hadn't left the planet earlier. This was a good thing for him, as it meant mostly clear skies for his travel to the bunker. Various news networks reported from the battle above. Darnell focused his attention on the fate of the Tri-cess (the three princesses who had been taken hostage aboard the *Nightmare*). He watched as the fate of his planet hung in the balance. The broadcast was being monitored by most of his planet's citizens right now as they awaited their fate.

Darnell's next task was to ask for Tyron. His computer recognized his request and directly connected the two via video chat. Tyron was in a traditional navy-blue and black robe. He hadn't changed the color of his clothing to represent the fragmented empire. He looked just as he always did, representing both sides of the conflicted Acolytes. "Tyron, we have to stop this."

"We have to see what shakes out in the battle."

"We can't just sit here and wait while our leaders battle it out. I have one million clones in a refugee camp with no bunker huddling around Goddess Medica. They'll be obliterated if debris falls directly on them."

"I can't stop a war to save one woman," Tyron replied.

"You will have to. If God-Wrath finds out his mother is dead, there will be nothing to hold back his fury. The planet needs you, Tyron. I'm getting reports that people are dying all over. Our cities are being ravaged by the spillover. The death toll is already mounting, and we weren't even in the direct line of fire."

"I'll see what I can do."

"Please, anything to stop this violence. God-Reign's wisdom shines on you, Tyron."

Darnell's guard interrupted, saying, "We have reached the bunker, sir."

The door opened, and Darnell was rushed down an incomplete but secure hallway. "There is no way to contact the outside world from this point," said the guard. "If you have any more phone calls, now is the time to make them."

"No, I've tried all I can. It's time to ride this out," Darnell replied.

# Chapter 26

Princess Ebony, Mercedes, and Raven proceeded to get dressed. They fussed with makeup while working with each other's hair. Raven picked out the dresses that they would all wear: simple, long gowns in differing colors. "What do you think of this one, sister?" she asked Dark Cleo.

"I don't know. You know I don't know about these things. I'm only here for security."

Raven frowned and then turned to Ebony, who seemed to dislike the colors. "You know I am partial to all white," Ebony said.

"It's not a wedding," Raven replied.

"You just don't want to wear your family's colors," Mercedes stated.

"You got that right," Raven replied. "Black is so dreary. I'm not trying to scare the poor clones."

"You have to represent your family. It's not a social visit," Mercedes said.

"I think it is," said Ebony. "Raven is looking to run away with a nice clone. With a big—"

"Don't make fun of my sister," Cleo said.

"Lighten up. We are just trying to have some fun," said Ebony.

"I'll wait outside." Cleo pulled her rifle up. She forced a smile as she looked at her sister.

Once she was gone, Mercedes asked, "Why is your sister such a bitch?"

"She is still sad about Braylon. I think I just remind her of our brother."

An awkward quiet entered the room. Ebony and Mercedes hugged Raven as a tear entered her eye. "Don't ruin your makeup, honey. You don't want to redo it again," Ebony said.

"You're right," Raven replied.

"Listen, I'll wear my family's dull green in a show of support, okay?"

"I guess I will wear the black."

"And I will wear the pink," said Mercedes. "Even though I hate it."

"I guess it's settled," said Raven cheerily. "Let's go help some refugees."

Meanwhile, Dark Cleo had made her way to the pilot's position at the front of the arrow-shaped frigate they were flying in. "Get out," she said to him. "I need to fly a little to clear my head."

Soon, escorted by three fighter ships on each side, the flotilla arrived at Planet Terry, a simple out-of-the-way farm planet. *At least this will be nice and easy. Nothing happens out here*, Dark Cleo thought. She began the ship's descent, and the fighters followed the frigate into the planet's atmosphere.

# *Chapter 27*

Skyfall and the head Keeper sat at opposite ends of the bridge. The head Keeper seemed enthralled with the craftsmanship of his people, and he pointed out every detail of its superiority.

"We gladly await your command, God-Wrath," Skyfall announced, happy to have cut off the bragging of the head Keeper.

"I have a new strategy. From what you have told me of what happened while I was gone, we need to unify the empire. I no longer think that the clones have to be saved. They need to be destroyed. We will no longer hold back our punches. This wonderous battleship will be the embodiment of our power. I have the perfect test for it. Our first mission will be to clean up my old mistakes."

Skyfall couldn't contain the smile on her face, and the head Keeper nodded in agreement at God-Wrath's comments on the ship's abilities.

"I used to protect two refugee colonies, one on Terry and the other on Emortono. We shall destroy them both. Death to the clones. Death to my previous mercy. Prepare the fleet for zero space. We will leave immediately."

# Chapter 28

Planet Terry was nothing but farmland: large fields of golden corn next to large farmhouses and barns. Large combines manned by clone workers dotted the fields. Dark Cleo felt relaxed as she looked over the monotonous landscape. It soothed her while she avoided thoughts of the recent past. She flew the shuttlecraft past the farms, toward a large, clear, rocky space. The contrast was stark where the red rocks began, and the area was dry except for a small stream that ran parallel to large holes in the ground that made a cutout circle. The refugee camp had its own small spaceport that sat on its reversed bottom. Below the spaceport was an upside-down pyramid that filled a large hole. It was supported by giant beams that marked north, south, east, and west. Each pole was designed in the traditional style of the region. Even though the planet mostly had the same culture, there were still subtle differences, which could clearly be seen on the poles.

Dark Cleo saw the markings light up for her landing, and she glided the shuttlecraft in. The escort fighters circled about, creating a protective perimeter in the atmosphere as the other half of the escort force stayed in space to patrol the planet. "Sister, is everyone ready?" she called out.

"Not yet. We need thirty minutes," Raven replied.

Cleo rolled her eyes and then gave the guards their positions. They had a small security team of eight trained guards, all loyal to Dark Reign and his family members. They wore a double-black military uniform with the dark family tribal symbol on the back. Cleo could see the camp's security force waiting outside, along with its administrator. Clones gathered behind the security guards, and their mixed chatter created a crowd noise that awaited the princesses.

Cleo lost her patience and proceeded to open the door into the shared living rooms. "We have a schedule to keep. Which one of you is the holdup?" she asked.

"Me," Mercedes replied.

"Hurry up, Mercedes."

"Just a few final jewelry touches, Cleo."

"Dark Cleo to you."

"Princess Mercedes to you."

They locked eyes for a second. Then Mercedes moved on, placing the last tiara on her head. Ebony activated three cameras, which floated in the air and followed the princesses as they started to line up after Cleo. "Ready," Mercedes said, and Raven and Ebony nodded in agreement.

Cleo opened the shuttle door to roaring applause from the crowd. Two security guards were already outside, coordinating with the local security. The remaining guards assigned themselves to the princesses. They appeared to have favorites based on how much luggage and supplies they had to carry. The three remaining guards had to unload supplies from the ship and hand them over to the camp. They unloaded food, water, basic clothes, and other supplies the princesses had brought with them. The cameras flashed as reporters from all over the galaxy took pictures and asked for interviews. "Can we speak with you? Do you have any words to say?" a young man asked, his chest clearly marked with a media badge.

"We are only here for the refugees," Raven replied, leading the princesses past the media.

"It's the Tri-cess! The three princesses!" a voice could be heard yelling in the crowd as he tried to get closer. He fought with other reporters and security, but he did not succeed in getting past the crowd.

"This way," Cleo ordered. Everyone crowded into an elevator. "Which would you like to inspect first? We have to be back on the ship within five hours. Until then, Raven, it's your show."

"I want to see the worst camps. They need our help the most," Raven replied. The other princesses smiled in self-assured agreement. "We are going to do a lot of good this day."

"But that's on the bottom level, outside the pyramid. It's not in the authorized areas," Cleo replied.

"We are not babies, and we won't sit at the kiddy table," said Ebony.

"We won't do any good if we don't help the neediest," said Mercedes.

"Is it my show or not?" said Raven. "Because, if it is, we are going to the bottom to help those who can't even get an apartment inside the pyramid."

"They are not apartments. They're cells," Cleo clarified.

"Whatever. You know what I mean."

"Fine. It's getting stuffy in here anyway." Cleo gave her men a look, and they checked their weapons. They carried large stun rifles that were capable of knocking people unconscious with a single shot and of firing rapidly. The guards felt confident that they could handle any scenario that popped up while they were in the camp's lower level. Cleo worried that they were overconfident because there were thousands of refugees and only a couple of them. She had issued everyone a lethal sidearm except for the princesses, just in case anything got out of hand. Finally, she pressed the button, and they all descended past the administrative offices and the lower levels of the inverted pyramid.

They descended down the middle of the pyramid until they reached a rectangular shaft made out of frosted glass. It poked out of the top of the inverted pyramid, and they kept going down. Another ten feet, and the elevator shaft came to an end. The doors opened, and they were greeted by unmanned, ragged tents scattered about. The refugees huddled around various small pit fires. The princesses clashed against the rocky, rugged canyons, hills, and caves that the refugees lived in. Most people looked at the princesses and started to walk towards them. The guards fanned out and circled the princesses, their crowd-control stun rifles raised and at the ready. Most clones didn't react to their presence but continued to share stories and talk amongst themselves.

The princesses shared an offended look. Raven looked to Ebony and then to Mercedes, who both looked just as confused. Turning to engage the refugees, she grabbed a megaphone and decided to make an announcement. "We have food, water, and other supplies to hand out—"

Cleo snatched the megaphone from her and shouted into it, "Line up in three single-file lines if you want to receive the supplies. Those out of line will not receive any supplies."

The guards went to work setting up a large table for the princesses to access the supplies and to act as a barrier. Men, women, and children started to gather from all around to reach the princesses and the free supplies they were giving away. Princess Mercedes gathered children in a group so she could take photos of them as she gave away water. Princess Ebony took pictures of herself giving out relief aid. "This is going to play well on the web. I'm so glad you talked me into this, Raven," she said. "Maybe our families can find us better husbands." At this, the princesses laughed. Several clones laughed hesitantly as well; they did not appear to get the joke, but they wanted to play along.

An older, muscular clone appeared. He had a sex clone designation tattoo on his face. His light skin was dusty from being unbathed. The clone walked up to the front of the line in a threatening manner. His brethren moved out of the way as he approached. Dark Cleo ran to intercept, and her guards had their guns pointed at this newcomer. "You need to go to the back of the line," she said.

He planted his feet in defiance. "I won't get any if I'm back there. We all know the supplies will run out."

The crowd overheard his warning and started to panic. Mercedes and Ebony moved back behind their guards, who started to threaten the crowd. The line collapsed, and a rush of people grabbed at the supplies, no longer waiting for their turn. "You, you started this," Cleo said to the man.

"I'm just trying to eat," he replied. She raised her stun rifle and pointed it directly at him.

"Stop!" yelled Raven. The crowd listened to her. "There is enough for everyone. We will make sure of it."

"That's not going to work, sister," said Cleo, still holding the man at bay with her rifle. His hands had balled into fists.

"Stop it. They are just scared," Raven begged. Cleo didn't move her finger, ready to pull the trigger.

Raven suddenly pushed her way towards her sister and the detained man. His eyes moved from despair to fury, and he looked ready to take all of his life's frustration out on the Acolyte who stood in front of him. Raven positioned herself in front of Cleo and pushed the gun's barrel to the side so that it no longer pointed at the defiant clone. It discharged a stunning bolt, hitting a random child. This was an invitation to her men to open fire. They suddenly started to fire round after round of stunning lasers. People were falling over each other as they suddenly collapsed to the ground. A human stampede moved away from the security guards and back into the hills. People slipped and fell trying to get away.

"Tell your people to stop this at once! Tell them it's safe!" Raven ordered Cleo.

"I can't. We have to keep you safe!" Cleo yelled.

"You are killing my people," the man said from his position behind Raven.

"We are here to help. Not to do this. Have your men stand down, or I will follow the clones," Raven stubbornly demanded. She moved backward and fell into the man behind her before Dark Cleo could grab her and force her back towards the elevator against her will.

Cleo assessed the situation. She looked around and then ordered over the radio, "All units stand down." They stopped firing.

"Get doctors and nurses down here," Raven demanded.

Twenty minutes later, the area had been secured, with local security forces making a perimeter. "We were really lucky, princess," said the local doctor. "No one was seriously injured. We are able to patch everyone up and get them back to their tents in no time." He looked pleased with himself and self-assured.

"I am so glad. I would have been devastated if we'd ended up hurting people," Raven replied.

"I don't know what you were thinking, Cleo," said Mercedes.

"I was thinking I didn't want three dead princesses down underneath a pyramid. And for the last time, it's Dark Cleo."

"It should be Baby Killer Cleo," Ebony said.

"That's not fair to my sister," Raven replied.

"Pack up your things," said Cleo. "We are going home."

"No, we're not. We still have five more spots to pass out supplies," Raven said as she moved her hands to her hips.

"You can't be serious," Cleo replied.

"Dead serious. We aren't leaving until these supplies get into the hands of the people who need them."

Raven turned and moved towards the defiant clone. He still stood in the same position. She handed him a full care package, all the supplies he could need for a week. Then she asked, "Are you able to calm your people for the rest of our visit? We have enough for everyone."

The man nodded. She smiled in return. She looked at Cleo and said, "Let's go." And this time, she led everyone up the hill to the new distribution spot.

# Chapter 29

"We have arrived," Skyfall announced as they hovered over Planet Terry. The full fleet appeared out of zero space and orbited the planet.

"We are receiving a report that a group called the Tri-cess is on the ground and is distributing supplies to the clone refugee camp," said the communications officer, one of the Keepers. "The Tri-cess appears to comprise the three most eligible princesses. They have not been betrothed to any family to strengthen an alliance yet."

"Excellent. I want them put under my protection, Skyfall," said God-Wrath. "Go to the planet and rescue them. I can use them to strengthen my empire once it is unified. They will make an excellent prize for the loyal families."

"One of the Tri-cess is Dark Reign's daughter. He'll never surrender her," Skyfall replied.

"Then you better capture her soon, before she escapes."

Skyfall saluted and then left the bridge. Taking a Keeper strike team, she departed for the surface.

"Sir. We have reports of fighters returning to the surface and a battleship appearing from the other side of the planet," the communications officer reported.

"Just one?" God-Wrath replied.

"Yes, sir."

"If they are foolish enough to take up arms against their God, blast them out of the solar system."

# Chapter 30

Mycelia sipped her purple, iridescent drink. It smelled of sweet nectar and it was strong enough to clean the windows. "The civil war is weakening your position," she told Tyron.

He barely smiled in reply. "Have you come here to brag? Or to welcome me into the club of former great empires?"

"It's not like that," she said.

"Then what is it like?" he asked. He started to pace around his room, looking at the trophies, the self-congratulations of peace bestowed by and for the Acolytes. He stopped in front of a great wall that had all the flags of the families. He tried to reconcile what he should do to stop all of them from fighting with one another. *They will destroy me*, he thought.

"I'm creating a peacekeeping force," said Mycelia. "The CDF will be its vanguard. Even with our more advanced firepower, we just don't have the numbers to make it incontestable. I still need your permission."

"You mean to occupy us? Like some third-world planet? The balance of power would be too off-center. I could never allow this."

Mycelia finished her drink and then poured another. She got up and raised her eyebrows, looking to another glass.

"No thanks. I can't keep up with you," Tyron replied.

"Neither can your government. Not while the families fight each other."

"That was a cheap shot."

"The situation is getting too desperate to hold anything back."

"I can take this to the emergency tribunal. I doubt it will gain any traction. Everyone is too focused on grabbing territory and crimes of opportunity."

"The peacekeepers I am putting together will help with that. They will be able to monitor acts of aggression by any opportunistic families," Mycelia proudly exclaimed.

"You are all too happy to rub this in my face. Next, you will be telling me the independent planets are going to ban together and create one big happy peacekeeping armada.

"That's exactly what I am saying."

"I think you have had too much to drink," Tyron said, turning his back to the wall of many families.

"You don't know my limit. I don't have one," said Mycelia.

"It's time for you to leave." Tyron motioned for his guards to return to the room.

"The Acolytes need a helping hand. We will give it to you. All you have to do is just ask." With that, Mycelia was escorted by Tyron's guards back into the hallway.

# Chapter 31

The *SKS*, an old battlecruiser, came into full view of God-Wrath's intimidating Keeper fleet. Its crew knew that there was no way to fight the sheer number of ships the opposing fleet was made of. The ship moved into a stable orbit above the refugee camp, making it the sole barrier between the armada and the princesses below. If they could get in the way long enough, maybe the group down below could make preparation and escape. The ship flew in defiance of all orders to stand down and join the Keepers in support of God-Wrath's new order. The old crew had proven themselves to be just as stubborn as the old battlecruiser they manned.

A dropship appeared with an escort of fighters and bombers protecting it. The weapons of the *SKS* were ready and aimed in the dropship's direction. The ship and its escort flew directly at the *SKS*, not stopping or slowing down.

"This is the captain of the *SKS*. Keeper dropship, we ask that you change course. This planet is under the protection of Dark Reign, and we answer only to him. Turn around and take your fleet with you."

Nothing.

*Looks like we are in a game of chicken,* the captain thought. *This presents me with no good options. If I fire, the whole armada will attack. If I don't, I fail my duty.*

"Sir, we are registering a huge spike of power coming from their flagship," the old and trusted first officer reported.

"Put it on the main screen."

Two large disks on the underside of the flagship started to glow. What looked like strikes of lightning transferred between them, and they were gaining in number and strength with each second. "The dropship will be in range in ninety seconds," the first officer reported.

"Launch our fighters. I don't want it to have an easy time getting to the ground," the captain ordered. "As soon as—"

A blue bolt of an incredibly powerful laser flew above the descending dropship, blowing up the *SKS* in one blast. Several of its fighters were too close and were caught in the blast. Several others surrendered once they found out that they were without a support ship. They pledged their allegiance to God-Wrath and let the dropship approach without harm.

"Now that that's out of the way, let's go princess hunting," Skyfall told her group of soldiers as they entered the atmosphere. This elicited a round of laughter from her men. "Remember, they are not to be harmed, but anyone who takes up arms against God-Wrath deserves their judgment. Am I clear?"

"Yes, Mistress," they responded.

# Chapter 32

"We need to go now!" Dark Cleo yelled as she grabbed Raven and rushed away from the makeshift supply center. She pulled Raven with a firm grip.

"No, we have two more sites today," Raven said, resisting.

"Don't argue. We don't have the time." Cleo started to pick up the pace as she moved closer to the elevator. "Let's round it up, men," she ordered. "Fast extraction protocol. If the princesses give you too much grief, stun them."

"Wow, it must be serious. You've never threatened to do that," Raven observed.

"It's bad." Cleo let go of Raven, leaving a welt where her hand had been. "Move, move, pick up the pace," she ordered. The princesses lifted their gowns above their ankles so they could run without tripping over their own clothing.

Clones rushed in the opposite direction, towards the unmanned supplies. The soldiers had abandoned their old mission of keeping order, and they circled the princesses and lined up behind Dark Cleo. She gave them a nod and told them to open fire on anyone who came between them and the elevator.

"Stop," said Raven. "They aren't doing anything wrong."

"Trust me, they have a much bigger problem than us right now," replied Cleo.

The light of the pyramid went black, and emergency lighting gave the dirty canyon a soft glow. The frosted glass of the elevator went black, and then it turned back on like a beacon.

Huffing and puffing, they all felt like their lungs would hop out of their chests as they ran towards their only escape. Small explosions and loud bangs could be heard above them. Earth and rock fell from above, filling the air with dust. The princesses looked just as desperate to get out of the situation as any other. Dark Cleo looked back, surprised that the princesses were keeping pace—a miracle considering they were in fancy high heels. Cleo knew her sister was not into physical fitness, but she was impressed that she did not have to slow down for Raven and her friends to catch up. *The danger has brought a new sense of urgency to the spoiled brats.*

Debris from an explosion fell into the space between the canyon and the inverted pyramid. A flash of light lit up the canyons as huge chunks of metal poured down, hitting anyone and anything in their path.

Finally making it into the elevator, Dark Cleo quickly closed the door after the important members of her party had made it inside.

She pushed the keypad for the top floor. As the elevator ascended, Raven, Mercedes, and Ebony huddled together in one corner, while Cleo's men stood in the other, catching their breath. The princesses took off their shoes and threw them in the corner. "They won't do us any good," said Raven when she could finally breathe normally for a second.

"Is everyone okay?" asked Dark Cleo. "Princesses? Squad?" Both groups nodded in acknowledgment. "Great. Stick close to me. I won't let anyone harm you or your friends."

The elevator stopped, jolting everyone inside. Cleo tapped her communicator. "Minister Tyler, it's Dark Cleo. You are in charge of this facility. If anything happens to the Tri-cess it's on you. Now get this elevator online." Alarms started to sound in the background.

"I'll send a team."

"A team? That's not good enough."

"Security will be there as soon as they can. Just let me check which team is free." The voice on the other end went quiet for what seemed like a year. Everyone in the elevator stared at Dark Cleo, closely listening to her side of the conversation. "No team is free. I can't spare anyone. I'm sorry, Dark Cleo.

You will need to find a way out of there yourself. The administration is evacuating. No one is coming."

"Fine, we don't need you. My father will hear about this, Mr. Tyler."

"I'll gladly face him if any of us make it out alive," the minister replied, and he cut the communication.

"They aren't coming, are they?" said Raven.

"What will we do?" Mercedes asked, panicked.

Dark Cleo popped open the panel behind the console. "Give me your kit," she ordered one of her guards. He complied, handing her a small, sturdily built datapad. It was made of a hard-plastic enclosure, and two prongs poked out. She hit a button, and it shot the prongs into the panel, connecting with the wires behind. Cleo quickly tried to override codes and divert power to the elevator, but she did not make any progress. "Shit, this isn't working. Did you test this out? Is it broken?" She balled her fist and punched the elevator.

"Move over," Princess Ebony commanded. She grabbed the device from Cleo and proceeded to click through red screens, quickly turning them green.

"How are you doing that?" asked Cleo.

"I'm good with electronics. I had to take something in school, and my family has always been on the technical side of things. We can't all be warriors," Ebony replied as the last red code turned to green. There was a surging sound, followed by a pop. The elevator lit up and started moving again.

"Thanks. I think I have a new respect for you," said Cleo.

"Save it. Just get us out of here!" Raven cried in the background. Tears poured down her face as Mercedes comforted her.

"Why are you crying?" one of the guards asked.

"Because so many people are dying," Mercedes replied, and she was soon crying along with Raven. They wailed as the elevator ascended.

Cleo looked at her sister and balled her fists again. She turned towards the door and waited. Shaking her head, she looked back and tried to find some words to say. She couldn't, so she turned back and stared forward. *I'm going to do my part*, she thought.

The elevator came to a stop, and its door opened. Dark Cleo and her group were welcomed by the sounds of fighters battling each other above their heads. They looked around to see the crashed remains of one of their escort ships. Its lower section was on their left, and its cockpit on their right. The pilot was hunched over in his seat, dead. A female clone blocked the path to their ship. She stared at them with the haughtiness of an imperial. She was flanked by five soldiers on each side. Cleo could tell that they were Keepers. Their patchy skin and unique robes were hard to miss. They all held rifles, which were pointed directly at Cleo and the band of princesses she was trying to protect.

"Skyfall," Cleo whispered, stating the obvious.

"Do you worship the new God?" asked Skyfall.

"That is a definite 'No' from me," replied Cleo. "How about you, boys?"

"We only take orders from Dark Reign," the soldier next to her replied.

"Tri-cess?" Cleo asked.

"Umm, we are with you," replied Raven. "Who's the clone?"

"I'm the Acolyte of God-Wrath. I shall render his judgment upon you." Skyfall whistled, and blaster fire immediately followed. Stun bolts answered, but Dark Cleo's men were outgunned.

"Use your sidearms!" Cleo demanded.

Her group of guards and princesses took cover behind the ship wreckage. It was too late for two of her men. They perished just as they realized that the stun bolts had no effect on the Keepers' armor, which had been hidden under their robes. Cleo took her gun, aimed at Skyfall, and fired.

# Chapter 33

Dr. Tom felt big. He felt smart. He'd just upgraded his ship's stealth technology. *This upgrade makes the stealth drive state-of-the-art. No one will ever know I'm there, even if they run right into me.* Confident of his new achievement, he inspected the cloaking drive. It looked like a server rack on his small ship. He pushed the thoughts to his machine men counterparts, who pushed back with contentment. They were proud of him, and he loved it.

Then he felt a new push, one telling him they had almost reached the artifact: a very old shielded observation station around a sun. *Only four years until the alignment,* he thought. He pushed out thoughts of getting a prepared rush in. They needed to do this quickly.

They docked at the massive observation station. The airlock opened, and the machine men rushed in, quickly overrunning the research and security teams. The machine men crushed the heads of anyone they found, whether they tried to resist or not. They showed no mercy and did not discriminate. Anyone with a pulse needed to be eliminated.

The last few archaeologists fled from the machine men, locking themselves in the main control room. Dr. Tom pushed violently. *They can't be allowed to signal for help, or we are doomed. This observation station is located in the middle of an occupied solar system. If the residents find out there is any threat to the station, they'll just blow it out of the sky. A machine man in space is a fate worse than death.*

He examined the locked metal doors and the ancient markings, which were written in a forgotten language in a brownish-iron color that stood out. He hadn't seen anything so arcane in quite a while. Then he noticed the weapons left on the floor. They were easily capable of blasting through unshielded doors and then finishing off the remaining flesh bags.

Dr. Tom pushed more thoughts to his machine men: *Pick the weapons up and finish this.*

*Yes, sir,* they replied, but their response did not turn into action. The machine men just stood there, blank.

He pushed again. *I know it's locked, but just pick up the weapons.*

*We can't,* they replied.

He pushed harder, trying to override their thoughts with his own. They resisted, their minds responding by creating a hive defense and locking Dr. Tom out. "Fine, I will just do it myself. Like a barbarian," he said. Picking up one of the guns, Dr. Tom blasted the locking mechanism of the control center.

Inside the room were a man and a woman. "Please don't. We don't have anything of value. We are just archeologists. We are not a threat!" the man yelled at him.

Dr. Tom did not respond. Instead, he pulled the trigger, burning the man and woman. "That handles that," he said. "Now it is time to use this thing for its real purpose."

Dropping the gun to the floor, he went to work on the computer systems. He tried to read the archaic menus and navigate the screens, but the panels did not respond to his touch. He looked at the burned couple in front of him and thought, *That won't do.*

Dr. Tom could feel the machine men pushing thoughts to him once again, and he could communicate with them as well. One of his compatriots pushed him an image of a completed observation platform. *Where did you find this?* he asked. An image of a headless man appeared.

*Just down the hall,* Dr. Tom thought. He moved. *I have to see this in person.*

The lifeless body lay before him. *You won't need these,* he thought, and he ripped the body's fingers from its hands and attached them to his own. He picked up a hand-drawn piece of paper that showed a huge missing section and an address to an ancient museum. *I know where that is*, Dr. Tom thought. *This is going to take a lot more work than I expected.*

# Chapter 34

The war council was set up in haste in the belly of the *Nightmare*. The room's high ceiling made an imposing presence. The door was being reinforced as they met. Tyron approached the reigning military heads, surprised that representatives of the ruling families were not present. *Perhaps they feel that the integrated military is non-biased*, he thought.

"I'm sure you are wondering where everyone is?" Dark Reign said from his seat in the middle of the semicircular table. "The families have entrusted us with making the military decisions from now on. They rule the people. We rule the ships."

"I couldn't agree more," said Tyron.

"What is this proposal from the league?" asked Vice Admiral Terrell, a deceptively friendly-looking man.

"I will just come out and say it," Tyron replied. "They want us to accept a peacekeeping force. And with the updates coming out of Planet Terry, I'm not sure if I disagree anymore, as dangerous as that seems."

Dark Reign slammed his hand on the table. "That won't happen. The council didn't take over the military just to hand it over to foreigners. I'd rather have Devante's traitorous ass shit on my grave."

"I think we should give this serious consideration," said Vice Admiral Maurice. "We can improve our position in the international community if we accept a little help. Dark Reign, you are the leader of this council, but you are not the only vote."

A man ran into the room, his cheeks flushed and his dark skin sweaty. "I have important news," he announced.

"What is it?" Dark Reign asked.

# Chapter 35

Skyfall rushed to remove the smothering armor from her body as she watched her Keepers engage the security forces. She grabbed the composite chest piece with one hand and tossed it at Dark Cleo, laughing as she fired multiple rounds of small metallic balls at its back.

Dark Cleo fired her blaster at the oncoming armor, but her shots had no effect. It hit her position and then exploded on impact, launching Cleo back. She fell behind cockpit debris, which hid her from Skyfall's view.

"Finish the rest off," Skyfall commanded.

The Keepers eagerly complied, firing rapidly at the remaining security forces until they could surround them. With their backs exposed, the guards surrendered, giving up their weapons. Raven, Mercedes, and Ebony were captured.

"Sorry to do this to you, ladies," said Skyfall. "Your sacrifice will make it so that many clones will no longer have to be bought and traded like you will be."

"My father will make you pay!" Raven yelled. Mercedes and Ebony cried as they were herded into their own ship.

"He will try," Skyfall replied.

# Chapter 36

"God-Wrath, we have received a signal from Skyfall. She was successful," said the communications officer.

"Good," replied God-Wrath. "Time to see how well this flagship performs. Test its main weapon on that clone camp. Also, destroy their capital city for sending that ship to confront us. I need to get my house in order."

The large disk on the underside of the ship charged up once more. It sparked and glowed, lighting up space around it.

Down below, the residents of Planet Terry could see a glow emanating from the sky. It looked as though a star were forming.

The ship shot a light-blue beam at the refugee camp. It was a direct hit.

\*\*\*

Dark Cleo looked back at the camp. She saw the beam of blue light create a small dust cloud. Then there was an explosion that blocked everything else out. For a moment, she could not hear or see anything; she was a passenger in the experience of this explosion and then the hiccup of the planet responding to being punched so hard from space.

When she came to her senses again, she looked back, glad she had found an emergency jetpack from the fighter wreckage. She jetted off in a random direction. She needed to find a spaceship and get back into the action. She was not going to sit around and do nothing while her sister was a captive. *I have to get her back*, she thought.

# Galactic Mandate: A Radical Cause

The second beam of blue light speared the sky, and a second explosion occurred, this time in front of her, in the city that was her destination. The destruction this time was worse than before. She stopped flying and landed in a cornfield. With destruction both in front of and behind her, she could only stop and rest. She looked around and saw a large barn. She walked to it, and there, she found a bunch of scared clones huddled around the equipment. They feared the end but offered refuge, motioning for her to join them.

"Come, young lady. You are going to be safe with us."

# Chapter 37

"It's the princesses, sir," one of the bridge officers announced to Dark Reign. "They have been captured, including your daughter."

"What about Dark Cleo?" Dark Reign asked.

"She is missing, presumed dead in the devastation."

The council erupted in chatter as its members fought to be heard.

"Enough. These proceedings are over," Dark Reign announced.

Tyron's head lowered, and his shoulders slumped.

"No, they are not," said Terrell.

"If you can't protect your own daughter in this time of crisis," said Maurice, "we need to consider the offer presented by Tyron."

"I say we put it to a vote," said Terrell.

"I've already decided it. No peacekeepers," said Dark Reign.

"I vote to override," said Terrell.

"You have my vote," said Maurice.

The room looked to the last two remaining vice admirals, Darius and Malik. They raised their hands in agreement. "We have it four to one, enough for an override," Terrell said.

"This is a mistake. Trust me," said Dark Reign.

"Time for me to make the arraignments," Tyron said. His head held high, he left the room.

# Chapter 38

Dozens of CDF ships appeared over Emortono. The peacekeeping force that Tyron and Mycelia had agreed upon went into orbit around the planet, creating a line of warships in front of the defense platforms. Interns, secretaries, and random officers scurried about, and alarms sounded, but they were quickly turned off.

"What is this? You said only a peacekeeping force was supposed to show up, not this armada," Dark Reign said to Tyron via a video chat session.

"This isn't what we agreed to," replied Tyron, "the full CDF Fleet above Emortono."

"They are acting like they own the place. You have sold us out."

# Chapter 39

"What are your commands?" Skyfall asked God-Wrath.
He gripped his command chair and leaned toward her. "I bet everyone is ready for me to give the reunification command. To take back our capital and then finish the cause. But first, I've got a detour in mind."

"We are not going to Emortono?" Skyfall asked.

"No, we are not. I have just a small detour to strike at the heart of the pretender. No one rules my empire without paying a price. Set a course for Planet Midnight."

"But that's the Dark Family's home. How will that help us destroy the CDF?" Skyfall asked.

The room fell silent as God-Wrath took notice. "It seems I'm not the only one who has changed. You now question my commands and my judgment?" Skyfall looked down. "Input the coordinates and go," God-Wrath ordered.

Skyfall gave the command, and all the warships entered zero space after agreeing on their new destination.

Planet Midnight was a dark planet with only four hours of sunlight. It was mostly heated by volcanic activity. The citizens used the volcanoes to power their massive cities. A very modern planet, it held some of the most metropolitan citizens of the Acolyte Empire. The geometric lines of light and patterns lit up the dark side of the planet, obscured only by its defense platforms and garrison fleet.

The fleet of Keeper ships directly engaged the warships in their way. "Ready the main cannons. Slice open the Dark Family's fleet once we have the disk charged," Skyfall ordered.

"Cancel that order," said God-Wrath. "Let the fleet handle those ships. We will need the energy for a bombardment campaign."

"But there are no clones down there, just your civilians," Skyfall replied.

"They shouldn't have supported Dark Reign in his rebellion," the head Keeper said.

"They don't," said Skyfall. "Let me conquer the planet humanely and justly. I'm sure the citizens will see your light and worship you as I do."

"They had their chance," replied God-Wrath. "Was it not you who had me tortured for months to get me ready for just this? I am no longer the naïve boy who went into that prison. I am the God my father never was. You wanted me to be ready and able to do whatever it takes to complete our mission of ridding the galaxy of the CDF. This is what it takes."

"I wanted you to do what was needed, not become a merciless monster."

"That's enough. Are you going to carry out my orders, or do I need to find a new admiral?"

"No, sir. I will ready the disk cannon for planetary bombardment on your command," Skyfall said, and then she left the room, her cape following behind her as she rushed away.

The head Keeper slithered his way to God-Wrath's side. "We have the three princesses with us. Why don't you marry one of them?"

God-Wrath rubbed his chin, pondering what he had just heard. This gave the head Keeper the impression that he should continue. "Let me bring them up. A wedding always brings up the morale of the crew."

The Dark Family fleet was quickly overwhelmed and the defense platforms were overrun by the sheer size of the Keeper fleet. God-Wrath and his bridge crew watched as the explosions filled their view. God-Wrath even heard a quick celebration from some of the crew members stationed about. The consolidation of his power was almost complete.

"Bring the Tri-cess to me, Keeper," commanded God-Wrath. "Your plan to boost morale is a good one. Pause the bombardment. I want my second marriage broadcasted across the galaxy."

"It will take a while to get them ready. Which one should we get in the wedding dress? Which of the remaining two should be bridesmaids?"

"I want Dark Reign's daughter ready to marry within the hour. I think marrying while her home planet sits as a backdrop is appropriate, don't you?"

# Chapter 40

"Sir, we have reports that Planet Midnight is under attack," Vice Admiral Terrell reported.

"Is it the main Keeper fleet?" Dark Reign asked.

"Yes, it is, sir."

"Great. Then we have a chance to split their forces and inflict some pain on their numbers."

"I was thinking the same thing."

"Get the fleet prepped for zero space right away," Dark Reign ordered.

Vice Admiral Terrell led him to the elevator. They both seemed to be brimming with nervousness as they strode briskly down the halls of the *Nightmare*. "I'm glad I have the fleet battle-ready," Dark Reign said.

"Did you enjoy your brief time off of the ship?" Terrell asked.

"Do you have a battle plan prepared?" Dark Reign countered as they entered the elevator.

"You have never been one for small talk. If we can get behind the fleet and coordinate with planetary defenses, we can hit them from two sides."

"Won't they have destroyed all of that by now?"

"I'm not talking about the defense platforms. I'm talking about what they actually have planetside. They won't be expecting it, because it's not enough to cause any serious damage. But it should be enough to drop shields so the fleet can pummel them."

Dark Reign's eyebrows grew closer together, and he rubbed his chin in careful consideration. "This should get the Keeper Fleet to panic," he almost whispered. "They haven't been in a fair fight yet. They should fold and crumble like the Imperial Guard did."

Terrell rocked back and forth on his heels, pleased that his plan was about to be implemented.

They reached the bridge, and looking out among the stars, Dark Reign observed the CDF peacekeeping fleet. "With the CDF acting as peacekeepers, we will be able to leave fewer ships behind," he said, and he gave Terrell a knowing nod. "Maybe I was wrong about them."

The other members of the council joined Dark Reign on the bridge. He thought about how he would have been happier if they had all been on their own ships, but there was no time for transfers right now; they had to get to zero space and go. The council members took their seats in the conference center behind the captain's chair, which Dark Reign occupied. The ship was dark, like his family name. Everything was made of various types of black plastic.

"The zero drive is counting down, sir," one of the young officers communicated from the front of the bridge. He sat at a command station viewing monitor, the glass of the bridge just beyond him.

"Get ready to engage on my command. I want the entire fleet in zero space at the same time. We will need precision on this," Dark Reign ordered.

"Yes, sir," the bridge crew replied.

Terrell, Maurice, and the other vice admirals turned on their monitors and coordinated with their ships, relaying Dark Reign's command. They looked at each other. Everyone was satisfied that they were going to engage their prior monarch soon.

# Chapter 41

Skyfall found herself escorting the three captured princesses to the ship's bridge. "Why are you in a black wedding gown?" she asked Raven.

"It's my family color, that's why."

"No, I mean why are you in a wedding gown at all?"

"What do you think? Why couldn't I be captured by someone who wasn't an idiot?"

Skyfall shoved Raven forward, through the doors to the bridge. "Here they are!" she shouted. Ebony and Mercedes rushed to help their friend return to a graceful stance. "What are you going to do with the Tri-cess?" Skyfall asked God-Wrath.

"Isn't it obvious?" he replied. "I'm marrying Dark Reign's daughter to help unify my empire. Or my holy realm, I should say." He slowly walked down the many steps from his chair. He was wearing his most impressive religious robes and was dragging a long cape—a colorful peacock among a harsh military background.

Skyfall's heart started to race. She looked around the room for anyone to recognize what was happening. No one seemed to notice the sudden pain she was in. "I object. You need the blessing from the heads of family," she said, the only thing she could think of quickly.

"I need no such thing," he replied. "The families need to fall in line, and this is the perfect way to show them their place."

"You are making a big mistake. You can't just marry Princess Raven and expect the other families to fall in line. They don't have any reason to." Skyfall's heart began to slow.

Her words had fallen heavily on God-Wrath, and she finally seemed to be making some headway.

Reaching the bottom of the stairs, God-Wrath made a fancy gesture with his hands. He stopped in front of Raven. "What do you think, Princess? How would you acquire the loyalty of the realm?"

"I already have it. Because I'm a good person," she said as she slapped away the hand.

The guards in the room jumped, but God-Wrath calmed them with another gesture.

"Big claims from a hostage," Skyfall said.

"Maybe it's just foreplay," God-Wrath replied.

Skyfall puckered her lips and balled her fists at her sides. God-Wrath rolled his eyes and shook his head at her. She grunted in frustration. "I can't watch this. Why don't you just marry them all? Marry all the princesses in the empire if you want!" She turned and left the room.

"How dare you leave this heavenly occurrence!" shouted the head Keeper. "Stop her!"

"Let her go," God-Wrath commanded.

"But she disrespects you on this holiest of days."

"Today, she gets to. I'm going to give her some time. I need her well rested for what's next."

"I'm not sure you understand."

God-Wrath turned his back on the princess and confronted the head Keeper, looking down on the man as he towered above him. "Be careful. I gave her a pass, not you."

"I apologize."

Pushing the man aside, God-Wrath walked back up the steps to his raised chair. Moving his cape aside, he sat and looked down at the assembled guests. "Skyfall gave me an idea. She is right. Why don't I just marry the lot? Get the other princesses ready, the one from House Green and that other one. I'm taking three brides tonight."

"My word," the head Keeper said.

All three princesses collapsed, wailing and crying. Guards rushed to their sides, and the princesses tried to fight them off. Men held their feet and arms as they dragged them away.

"Time to get them prepared again," the head Keeper commanded.

# Chapter 42

The countdown could be heard from every corner of the *Nightmare*. The bridge crew waited with nervous anticipation. This was going to be the fight of their lives. Vice Admiral Terrell had approved the last couple of details of his battle plan. He sat with the other vice admirals, giving them confidence. "Everything will go according to plan. They won't know what hit them."

The countdown stopped, and the ships suddenly jerked, rocking forward and backward. Alarms sounded, and the fleet reported.

"Dark Reign, everyone is reporting the same thing," said the communications officer.

A red, burning glow appeared above the CDF fleet. Wave after wave of the glow hit the ships protecting Emortono. "An interdiction field," said Dark Reign. "The damn CDF has trapped us here. Get me a line to Chancellor Judy now!"

"No need," one of the young officers replied. "We are receiving a transmission now."

"Put it up on the screen."

Chancellor Judy's smug face appeared. "Where do you think you are going?"

"That's none of your business. We are a sovereign nation. You will release our ships at once."

"Funny, because the way I see it, you are half a sovereign nation. I'm sorry, but you won't be going anywhere without my permission. Besides, what kind of peacekeeping force would we be if we just let you run off to make war on anyone you wanted?"

"You think this is funny? My daughters' lives are at stake."

# Galactic Mandate: A Radical Cause

"Well, I definitely can't let you leave. There is no way I can authorize a personal vendetta. I have an obligation to the galaxy here."

"We can force you."

"That you can, but I think you are smarter than that." The chancellor disconnected, leaving Dark Reign to look at an empty screen.

He hopped out of his seat and turned to stare at the council. "You, you did this."

"We didn't know this would happen," Maurice said. "I think the chancellor is actually right. We are headed off to what amounts to nothing more than settling a personal affair."

"Arrest them!" Dark Reign yelled.

The crew of the bridge looked at the war council and then at Dark Reign. Then they clearly picked a side. "Dark Reign is right. It's old men like you who are responsible. You got us into this mess," said an officer as guards surrounded the council.

"Take them to the brig," Dark Reign ordered. "Put them in a dark hole, because I don't want to see any of them again."

"Yes, sir," one of the guards replied. They handcuffed each member of the war council and took them away.

"What should we do now?" the officer asked Dark Reign.

He punched the wall and then ran his fingers through his hair. "We make repairs. If we can't bring the fight to God-Wrath, he'll bring it to us. The jolt of the interdictors should have scrambled everyone. Make sure the repair crews work double time. And send a message to all of the vice admirals. Inform them that the war council has been disbanded. It wasn't short-lived enough."

# Chapter 43

The flimsy door was knocked open by Skyfall's boot. The princesses rushed to cover themselves as they prepared under the watchful, gawking eyes of the guards.

"You!" Raven yelled. The princesses started to throw clothing and brushes and whatever was at arm's reach at Skyfall. She lifted her arm to protect herself from the onslaught of small projectiles.

"That's enough!" shouted a large female guard. Her voice echoed off the walls of the small, boxy, makeshift dressing room.

Skyfall continued forward and grabbed Raven by the ear. "I should kill you and wear your skin. I could do it, you know."

"Please, I have enough people who made themselves look like me. I didn't think God-Wrath's top general was just another creepy stalker. You would never pass the identification checks, anyway."

"We are at war. Do you think anyone is doing an identification check on a hostage princess?"

This affected Raven. "You are not going to do it."

"Watch me." Skyfall took a knife and raised it to Raven's throat. She could see the sweat on Raven's neck. She lifted a small drop off with the knife and flung it across the room, letting it disappear into nothingness.

The large female guard the princesses referred to as "the big lady" put a relaxing hand on Skyfall's shoulder. "I know you are hurting, but this is not the way. Trust me. God-Wrath may give you more leeway than any clone deserves, but he wouldn't forgive this."

"There is precedent. It's been done before," said Skyfall.

"That's in the history books," the big lady replied.

Skyfall released Raven, whose eyes were watering. The princesses embraced each other. Skyfall pointed her knife first at Ebony and then back to Mercedes. "He doesn't need either of you." She backed off and stormed towards the door. "You have thirty minutes," she barked.

Time passed slowly as she waited outside. She could hear crying, then the big lady comforting the princesses, and finally, she heard only silence when the time drew near. She could tell there was a general acceptance from the room beyond.

The head Keeper came from the hallway. As always, he admired and inspected every inch of the ship while he slowly walked down the hall. "God-Wrath is ready."

"I'm sure he is," Skyfall replied. She knocked on the door, this time giving it a much lighter touch than before. "Time's up."

The princesses came out of the room, all in matching wedding dresses, the only difference being the color of each. Each lady was draped in her family's colors. "I wonder who will give away Mercedes," asked the head Keeper. "There isn't anyone from her family on the ship."

"I will," said Skyfall.

"Unprecedented. A clone giving away not only one bride but two. You aren't even a family head."

"It's a sham anyway. What does it matter?"

"Well, I guess you have a point," the head Keeper replied.

Skyfall raised an eyebrow in surprise. "Let's walk these ladies down the aisle."

"You don't have to," Ebony said.

Skyfall laughed. "Oh, I do. I would rather float you ladies into space, but you know how much my opinion matters right now."

"Maybe we can make this an opportunity to talk some reason into God-Wrath," said Raven. "We can use our new position to become a voice of reason."

"I've literally tortured the man. If I can't tame him, the three of you have no chance," Skyfall said proudly.

The princesses looked away in an awkward silence.

"I'm sure a royal Acolyte can do better than a clone. Trust me, she isn't that special." The head Keeper winked at the ladies.

"I don't know if I can go through with this," Raven said as she slowly followed the head Keeper.

"Don't let that clone get into your head," the Keeper replied.

Skyfall folded her arms and huffed, ignoring the hate-filled comments.

The group approached the bridge once again. The ship was aligned with Raven's home planet, which was clearly visible from the bridge. Its lighted cities brought a sense of order to the planet's darkness. God-Wrath left his chair and approached the procession. He walked past the three princesses and to the glass of the bridge, close enough to touch it, and he looked intensely at the planet below. The head Keeper took his place; as minister, he stood behind God-Wrath, leaving room for the princesses to follow. Raven was nudged in the right direction.

"I won't do it," she said. "Hear me and listen to me. If anyone is watching this, this is against my will. I won't do it. I won't marry him." The other princesses quickly followed suit.

"Looks like this plan has failed. Follow me," said Skyfall.

"Not so fast," God-Wrath replied. "The wedding is just a mere formality. I could proclaim the marriages and be done with it."

The head Keeper whispered in God-Wrath's ear, "No, they must accept this. All three of them."

God-Wrath replied, "I'm pretty sure they won't."

"I heard them making plans to resist you while they were getting dressed," said Skyfall. "Give it up. It's a lost cause. Any planet that resists, I can just conquer for you."

"I know you will, Skyfall. You just don't understand how to woo a princess, though. It's a very delicate thing. It requires a strong man's intuition. Someone who can show dominance or maybe, just maybe, someone with the grace of a god. Fire!!!" Starting with a whisper, God-Wrath's voice gradually raised in volume until he was yelling.

# Galactic Mandate: A Radical Cause

The disk under the ship discharged a large blue beam that hit the planet below. It extinguished a huge portion of the light that came from the planet. Suddenly, an immense dark area appeared, a black mark amid the orange lines of light that marked the planet. "What about you, Ebony, is it? Right? Fire again!!!" he announced.

"No, please, stop it!" Raven yelled.

A quarter of the Keeper fleet aligned themselves with the planet and fired a bombardment of lasers in unison, extinguishing another portion of the light from the planet. It was easy to see from the bridge, and the ships looked so calm after they moved back to separate positions. "And you, Mercedes. Clearly, you have more sense than the rest? What say you?" he asked.

"Stop. I'll do whatever you want."

"You see. I don't think you understand. I don't think anyone on this bridge really understands. Skyfall, she opened my eyes. People only respect strength. They don't worship me because I'm a loveable god. They won't follow me into the abyss because I can see what they can't. This galaxy needs me. I have to show you the way. The new way. The CDF thinks they can resist, and so does Dark Reign, but that's not how it's going to be. Raven thought she could resist, and look where it got her. Resisting the word of God-Wrath is no longer an option. When I say there shall be no other power but mine in the galaxy, I mean it. When I say we shall no longer engage in the evil of cloning, it will no longer happen. And when I say I will marry three princesses who are so vain they call themselves the Tri-cess, I mean it. Fire, because this one is for you, Mercedes."

The right side of the fleet aligned to the planet. The glow of their lasers hit the planet, causing another section of lights to extinguish.

The princesses looked on, too terrified to speak. God-Wrath raised his arm in a challenge. "Who else wants to question my rule? Any usurpers in the room? Does anyone else want to openly rebel? This can happen to any of your homeworlds. This can happen to your homeworld, Mercedes.

Is that what you want?" She shook her head. "What about you, Ebony? Do you think your planet is safe from my wrath?" Ebony shook her head as well. "What about you, Keeper? Do you think because you provided this fleet that the rings are safe?"

"I-I-I assumed that you, that we would be in your good graces for such an act. My men would never turn on their homes."

"Is that right? All of the other Acolytes can run scared, but not the Keepers?"

God-Wrath turned, unbuckling his cape, which dropped to the floor. He rushed over to the unsuspecting head Keeper, gripping him in a headlock. The entire room suddenly erupted in a panic. The officers stepped back while the guards rushed in.

Skyfall brought up her weapons, eyeing the guards. "Don't try it. I will kill you and these princesses!" she yelled.

"Do you think you are immune? Do you think you are immune from my judgment?" God-Wrath asked the head Keeper.

Gasping for air, the old man was unable to respond. He scratched and clawed, trying to wrestle away from God-Wrath's grasp. "No, no, I'm not," he finally managed to say.

"Don't tell me. Tell your men," God-Wrath replied.

"Follow God-Wrath. His wisdom is all."

The Keepers stood down. They no longer looked agitated; the thought of any resistance had been swept away.

"Control the head Keeper, control the Keepers!" God-Wrath exclaimed. Letting go of the head Keeper, God-Wrath pushed him back towards his previous position in the room.

The man rubbed his neck and shrugged off the embarrassment. "Do you still want to be married by me, your holiness?" he asked.

"No, Skyfall will do it. She also needs to learn her place," God-Wrath said.

"But marrying the living God is reserved for the Keepers of the light. It is our highest honor," said the Keeper.

# Galactic Mandate: A Radical Cause

"Everything is what I say it is and nothing else," God-Wrath replied.

Skyfall bitterly lowered her weapon and moved to the Keeper's position, pushing him aside. She grabbed the book that was in his hand. It felt weird to be holding a real book. It was old and dusty. The head Keeper had everything bookmarked, so she didn't need to ask where to look for the information she sought.

"Get on with it, Skyfall," God-Wrath said.

"By the power of his holiness. By his graces and his divinity. I ask the par... I see that these three women have been given to God-Wrath as a tribute to greatness. He shall protect their worlds... like his own—"

"Or destroy them," God-Wrath said. He was now facing Skyfall and the head Keeper, who had taken a position behind her. The head Keeper tried to save some face by lending a guiding hand whenever he could. "Skip to this next part. I think God-Wrath wants this wedding to be over soon enough," he whispered.

"I, Skyfall, Admiral of the Divine Fleet provided by the Keepers of the Light, announce that you, God-Wrath, are now married to Princess Raven first, Princess Ebony second, and Princess Mercedes third. Their new names shall be Goddess Raven, Concubine Ebony, and Concubine Mercedes."

"What, we don't get the title of goddesses?" said Ebony.

"No, that only goes to the first wife," said the head Keeper in the background, happy to share his vast knowledge of the marital procedure.

Mercedes took her veil off, threw it to the ground, and stomped on it. "I'm married, but I don't have to be happy about it."

"No. I didn't require that, now did I?" God-Wrath replied. "Skyfall, lead the others to my quarters. Then prepare the fleet. We leave for Emortono within twenty-four hours. I have to let Dark Reign know he's my new in-law." God-Wrath chuckled.

"You mean, you want me to deliver his head on a platter," she replied.

Page | 173

"Yes, I do, Skyfall. Do you think the Keeper fleet is up to the task?"

"It better be." Skyfall turned and sneered at the head Keeper.

# Chapter 44

"We have received word that God-Wrath is headed here within the hour. I hope we can put yesterday's troubles behind us and work together in defeating him," Chancellor Judy told Dark Reign.

He sneered. *Either that or I will destroy you now to save myself the trouble of a fight, he thought.* "Of course, even though there have been some changes since I talked to you last, the peacekeeper fleet is still welcome. Together, we should wipe the floor with Devante's pompous return."

"That's what I like to hear. I am sure that once this mess is all over, I can count on your support in the Galactic League."

"I don't care what those screen watchers do. It's never affected me. If you want to sell clones and weapons, I'm not going to stand in your way."

"Good, we have an arrangement."

"If that's what you want to call it." Dark Reign ended the call. *I'm trading one pompous fool for another*, he thought.

An officer rushed in, yelling, "God-Wrath is coming! We have a fifty-minute ETA on his fleet!"

"Yes, I already know. Intelligence really needs to step it up. Who's in charge of it?"

"Well, it used to be God-Wrath," the officer replied.

"That explains it."

The officer lingered in the doorway. "Umm, sir?"

"What?"

"I'm not sure how to tell you this... He married your daughter, sir."

"WHAT?"

"Not just her. He married the entire Tri-cess."

"He—he can't do that. What about Dark Cleo?"

"No news, sir."

God-Wrath's only thought was to tear this officer apart. "Get out of here... now!"

The officer saluted nervously, then turned and left. Dark Reign looked out into space, enraged. *I will save my daughter at any cost. I need to clear my head. Maybe a call to Mother would help.*

"Call Mother and her band of hens," Dark Reign said to his computer console.

It beeped in error.

"I said, 'Call my mother.'"

It beeped again. He read the message on the screen. It said: "Location not found." *This can't be right.* He pulled up a feed from the satellite of his home planet. That was when he saw it: the devastation that was coming his way. His family home had been hit. Millions of people were dead. Whole cities had been destroyed. His eyes watered, and he threw things from his desk. Yelling and growling, he kicked and screamed wildly.

*Is God-Wrath going after everything I love? If he wants to play that game, I have his mother below. I should just swoop down and kill her. Maybe fire a shot from orbit just like him. No, that would be too easy. Striking at his family won't make me feel better. Or will it? What's the right thing to do, and how do I start protecting those I love? Is there anyone I love even left? I have to take something from God-Wrath, but what?*

# Chapter 45

"The Acolytes have authorized the peacekeeping force," Mycelia reported to Chancellor Judy.

The chancellor looked down at her from a holographic screen that was twice as large as Mycelia, her face filling the room. "Great. We are sending our entire fleet to Emortono. There, we will stop the menace of this new God-Wrath once and for all."

"But we are only authorized to send a small force made of a coalition of independent planets. They didn't say we could just occupy their capital."

"That is exactly what we will do. Don't ruin this accomplishment with naivety. I'll just consider this the nectar talking."

"My mind is clear. What you are doing is wrong," Mycelia replied.

"Stay in your cushy apartment in the league's space station while I do what needs to be done. After I occupy the Acolyte's capital, I don't think there will be much need for someone with your talents anymore. Better drink up while the supply lasts."

# Chapter 46

Chancellor, to what do I owe the pleasure?" Dark Reign asked.

"I wish I had better news," the chancellor said as she looked solemnly into the monitor.

"What intelligence does the CDF wish to share today?"

"God-wrath has returned. He seems to be amassing a sizable force to take Emortono. The CDF can give you significant information on when, where, and how to get a preemptive attack organized and implemented. With our combined forces, we can rout the enemy before they ever get it together." The chancellor seemed quite pleased with herself.

The various battle plans and other visualizations of the attack were displayed next to her image. Dark Reign studied them. "No," he said.

"What do you mean, 'No'? This is a golden opportunity to end your civil war. To rebuild your shattered government."

"I understand the stakes, but if he wants to attack me, let him come. I've got the moral high ground, and I don't need to cede it. I don't go attacking and killing. I'm not him."

"I see," the chancellor replied.

"All this scheming and politicking doesn't do anything. Let the best man be determined on the battlefield."

"Are we still allies?" the chancellor asked, taking what seemed like a new sales approach.

"We are," Dark Reign said, and he ended the call.

# Chapter 47

Dark Reign held his chest in panic. *I've already lost my son. I can't lose both of my daughters. I can't lose my whole line to this war*, he thought. Feeling too hot to breathe, he stripped himself of his uniform. Gasping for air, he sat at the desk in his home office. He dialed a direct connection to Death's Witness and waited for Michael to answer.

"What can I do for ya, Dark Reign?" asked Micahel. "You don't look so good."

"It's my daughters. One has been kidnapped, and the other is missing. I need you to bring them to me."

"Sure thing. Who kidnapped your daughter? And where was the other one last seen?"

"God-Wrath has them. He probably has them both." This was met with silence. Dark Reign looked into Michael's eyes via the monitor. "What is it? Do you know something?"

"No. I, ahem, just... We don't kill other Acolytes. I've told you that."

"I don't care about your morals. I want my daughters back."

"You will have to get them without us," Michael replied. "When you start killing your own, it never stops."

Dark Reign punched the monitor until it stopped working, hitting harder and harder with each blow.

"Stop!" Rear Admiral Wilson yelled. He had entered the room quietly. Dark Reign looked up, his eyes red and watering. "I know this is a painful time, but we have bigger problems."

"Not to me," Dark Reign replied.

"Maybe not. But you are the leader of the military, and we need you right now. Just as much as your little girls do." Dark

Reign ripped his shirt and wrapped the rag around his knuckles. "I mean no disrespect, but I have to show you the report from Planet Terry. It is nothing but complete destruction."

Wilson handed him a datapad with satellite pictures of a scorched planet. Dark Reign lifted the pad and swiped through the images, dragging his fingers across the screen, trying not to smear too much blood on it. He saw images of a destroyed city and a large hole in the ground. The image of what used to be a refugee camp. But he couldn't tell if it was nothing more than a tar pit.

"We have reports that God-Wrath is returning to Emortono. He is returning home to reunify the empire," Wilson said.

"Haven't we suffered enough?" Dark Reign asked.

"I also have a report from Tyron. Seems the peacekeeper act when through swiftly. We should be expecting a fleet in orbit soon."

"Just what I need. Move the *Nightmare* and recall every battleship loyal to the Imperial Navy. If God-Wrath wants a fight, I'm going to bring it to him. I don't care if I have to pull my daughters from his monstrosity myself."

"Do you think he would have the audacity to kidnap your daughters and then bring them back to you?"

"He's a fool. Fools do foolish things," Dark Reign replied.

# *Chapter 48*

Alarms blared, and officers rushed into the destroyed room. They looked around but didn't have any time to comment on the mess, although they did notice it. Still heaving from his tantrum, Dark Reign turned around. The window looked out into space. He saw the glow of the sun and the oranges, blues, greens, and tans of the planet below. Then he saw the purple-pink blips of light: the sign of ships appearing from zero space. Some smaller ships, even some frigates, had decided to test the interdictions of the CDF and slammed out of zero space. Their crews paid the price, as they drifted until the CDF fired its laser on them, creating a fireworks show to start the battle. The main fleet appeared far from the planet. Ships still appeared one by one. *The Keepers have been keeping a secret. I'll have to see how they created so many ships without my knowledge*, Dark Reign thought.

"You can see the battle has begun," a young officer said. His nametag read, "Officer Andre." Dark Reign's eyes moved to the CDF fleet. Its ships looked odd compared to his own. The peacekeeping force still circled the planet, but its ships moved to a form a defensive blockade. Dark Reign saw what he could take. *I know how I'll get my revenge*, he thought.

"Move the *Nightmare* and its escorts to the vanguard of the fleet," he commanded. "I want this ship to lead the attack. Prepare my shuttle. I'm going to lead from Rear Admiral Wilson's older ship."

"Are you running from combat, sir?" Officer Andre asked.

"Ha, no, this is above your paygrade, I'm afraid. Don't end up like the war council," Dark Reign warned. "Trust me. I have a plan. I'll lead the *Nightmare* by hologram. It will be like I'm there."

"The men... they are with you," Andre said reassuringly.

"I know they are. Let's see if I can get the people out of this mess God-Wrath and the CDF has created."

Dark Reign regained even more of his composure. *Maybe this will work*, he thought. *It won't make me feel better, but it will make him feel worse, and that's all that matters right now. Deception is not honorable, but sometimes, it's key. It's in the rules of war; no great battle was ever won without a bit of deception. If the tactic is good enough for our ancestors, its good enough for me. I am no better than they are.* He raced to change his clothes.

"Sir, have a little modesty," Andre requested.

"No time for that. Is the shuttle ready?"

"It is."

"The best cloak that we have?"

"You didn't say anything about a cloaking device. Why would you need that at a time like this? I think this is an all-the-cards-are-on-the-table kind of battle."

"You certainly are wise beyond your station, Andre. If we get through this, you are up for a promotion, but you haven't learned one of the most basic lessons, I see."

"What is that?"

"You always have something to hide. Now, go make sure the ship has a cloak," Dark Reign said as he pulled up his pant leg. He buttoned up a new shirt and made sure all of his metals and badges displayed correctly. *This is it. They need to see me as their composed leader. They can't see how much losing my daughters hurt. My family, my homeworld. Maybe this makes me stronger. I don't have much else to lose.* Finally done, he ventured down the halls of the *Nightmare*, looking up only from habit, as he knew the halls by heart.

Walking at such a brisk pace that it could have been called a slow run, he turned left, headed down a hall, and then turned right and into the elevator. When the elevator arrived at the proper floor, he left it, went down another hall, and entered the rear docking bay. There, he saw Andre talking with some other officers and inspecting a ship.

"This is the one," Andre proudly stated, rubbing off some dirt from an old swamp hopper.

"This piece of shit?" Dark Reign replied.

"You said you wanted a cloaked ship on short notice. This is will get you to the *LMR* in no time. Besides, you would stand out even in a cloaked ship if you brought something brand new over there. People talk, you know."

"I guess you do have a point."

"I know I do. Get in. We will take good care of your *Nightmare* while you are gone."

"I'm not going to be gone for that long. You'll be answering to my hologram in just a few minutes."

"Whatever you say."

Dark Reign got into the shuttle and closed the door behind him. He fiddled with the controls and then started a call. Punching in the codes, he had the *Nightmare* relay the call from its servers. *Voice-only should be fine.* "Chancellor, I need your ships to follow the *Nightmare* so we can take this battle to God-Wrath."

"I'm not sure we should do that. We are only here in a peacekeeping capacity. Making sure citizens can escape and commercial ships can still get out of the battle zone."

"We both know that if God-Wrath rolls over this fleet, you are next. He wouldn't even hesitate to give you a warning. You wouldn't have brought the entire clone defense force here if you were not trying to take him out."

"If we work together, I need you to understand how the hierarchy works. I'm at the top, and you are at the bottom."

"You can sit here and debate that all you want. Play politics. Invite him to a parlay for all I care. I'm the admiral of the Imperial Navy. Fighting battles is what I do. How many battles have your clones won against a force this size? I've been preparing my whole life for this. If you want to win, your ships follow mine. That is the way it's going to be. We can work the politics out later, because God-Wrath is not going to wait forever."

There was an awkward pause. Dark Reign waited patiently.

"We will follow your ships. Lead the way," the chancellor finally said.

"I'll have my officers send the coordination codes." Dark Reign turned on the ship's engines, entered the coordinates, and lifted off. *It's time to go slumming.*

***

The Keeper fleet held its position outside of Emortono, its sleek, new look clashing against the wildly disparate and merged fleets of Dark Reign and the CDF. Their ships started to separate as they formed an arrow that pointed directly at the Keepers. Support ships flew in between the well-organized Keepers. There was something distinctly missing. The massive battleship, the new flagship of God-Wrath, wasn't there. The Keepers had left a giant hole big enough for the battleship to park itself in. They flew around it like it was there, creating an optical illusion of an invisible force the Keepers could not touch.

***

"What are they waiting for?" the chancellor asked. She sat in a conference room in the middle of the free-for-all, surrounded by large monitors from which she could see the battle clearly. They displayed a wraparound view of the battle zone. The chancellor could see everything that was happening in real time in 360 degrees.

"I'm not sure, but from our intelligence reports, it looks as though the flagship is missing," said Robert Jones, the clone general. His face was tattooed with skulls where his identifier would normally be. The tattooed skulls had separate outlining colors, some red and black and others the inverse. It was a shocking feature to the otherwise entirely professional-looking man.

"Which one of these ships is the *Nightmare*?" the chancellor asked. Robert Jones pointed to the ship that was above and in front of their own, and that was followed by a contingent of battleships. "The Acolyte's flair for the melodramatic almost matches your own," she stated.

Robert smiled while selecting ships on his datapad, giving them orders to move closer or farther away. He held up his datapad to select a ship that was in sight of the room and issued an automated order by moving its image around on his device. "We should protect the *Nightmare* and abandon the planet," he said.

"Good suggestion, but that's not what we are going to do. We are going to break off and make a run for this missing flagship as soon as it appears. Either way, we will abandon this planet to its fate once it's done," the chancellor said in her most confident voice. "If we cut off the head, the rest will die. With our more advanced and superior weaponry, they don't stand a chance."

"No, they do not," Robert replied.

Another clone, who looked exactly like Robert, whispered in his hear, "Intelligence report. The Keeper fleet uses laser weapons. They say their weapons are even more advanced than our own."

"If the chancellor says we have the advantage, then we do," replied Robert. "It must be your report that is wrong."

"What was that?" Chancellor Judy asked.

"Nothing, just some useless information," Robert replied.

The Chancellor got up and surveyed the ships that surrounded them, turning her head so that she could take in all the information.

"Don't worry, Chancellor. You are in the safest spot in this entire battlefield," Robert said.

"I know, General. I know," said the chancellor as she looked off into the distance. She glanced at a group of older battleships at the tail end of the battle zone. "Looks like the Acolytes brought out some toys from the Genetic Wars." Everyone in the room laughed.

# Chapter 49

Skyfall stood over Raven and God-Wrath as they slept. She studied Raven's face, comparing their features. I should just take her place. It would be so easy. Just put my hand over her mouth, and no more Raven. Maybe it would be a curse and not a blessing. I would have to fuss with my hair, look beautiful at all times. Keeping up the action would just be tiring.

God-Wrath stirred, and Skyfall snapped to attention.

"Is it time already?" he asked.

"Yes, did you have fun consummating your marriages?"

"Don't start."

"It should be me. I should be these women."

"Yes, you should be," God-Wrath replied, pulling himself up and removing the covers. "Relax. They asked to be drugged."

"That doesn't make it better."

"The fleet, Skyfall, tell me about the fleet."

"They are already at Emortono and are holding their position. We should be there to lead the assault."

"Ha! Only the unimportant arrive on time," he said in his warmest voice, rubbing her cheek as he spoke. "When we make our grand entrance, that's when we enact the plan. I will singlehandedly stop cloning in the galaxy by my command."

Skyfall looked up at him with sterling-blue eyes, her fine black hair wrapping around his fingers. She pushed away and looked back at the princesses. "It doesn't look like they are going to wake up soon."

"Probably not. They will miss the glory that is to come."

"For the better. I think you gave them all they could handle last night." God-Wrath smiled at the thought. It was interrupted by a hard slap. "That's not what I meant. You murdered Acolytes."

Blood rushed to God-Wrath's face, shading it an even darker color. Not many people could tell when he blushed, but Skyfall could. "Are you embarrassed you killed so many of our people?"

"I'm doing it for you," he admitted.

"I don't want our people murdered."

"Acolytes are not your people. They are mine."

"Then my life is a lie?"

"No, it is not. You are one of us."

"I'm more Acolyte than you are."

"Maybe."

"I only want the completion of the cause. The end of cloning."

"No one should live through what our parents put us through," he admitted.

"Do you really have the vision to stop their practices? To change the society of the galaxy?"

"I do."

"Then let's go. The fleet needs us."

"We will have to kill many more of own kind before this is over. Can I count on you?"

"Yes. I will follow you into the abyss, but only if you remember why we are here."

"I do."

"This is not it," Skyfall said as she pointed at the sleeping women.

"Trophies. It's hard to keep so many families in line. They will help."

"They are good people. If you don't corrupt them."

"Power corrupts everyone. Even them."

"Let's get going. If we wait too long, the battle will start without your holy blessing, as the Keepers would say."

God-Wrath gave her a final smile as he got dressed. He was in his golden robes. A special wardrobe for a special occasion, the Keeper had instructed. God-Wrath knew he was right.

The head Keeper waited outside of God-Wrath's bedroom with a large group of religious people, the most devoted of the Keeper order. They chanted while others touched God-Wrath lightly as he passed. Skyfall followed closely behind, giving a menacing look to any Keeper who got too close to her. Slowly but surely, they made their way to the bridge of the ship. God-Wrath walked up the steps to the throne the Keepers had made for him. The religious Keepers scurried about and returned to their church.

"Head Keeper," God-Wrath called.

"Yes?"

"I never asked. What do you call this monument to rage?"

"I beg your pardon?"

"This ship, what is the designation of this ship?"

"The *Resolute*. That's the designation we gave it."

"That won't do. Maybe something that strikes fear into my enemies."

"We could name it *Desolation*."

"That is too literal. I've got it. *Desolution*. I decree that ship should be called the *Desolution*. Skyfall, go have the designation changed."

"Yes, sir," Skyfall replied. She moved to a computer terminal, typed in passwords, and changed it immediately under the watchful eye of the head Keeper. He treated his fleet with so much pride that he wanted to make sure every detail was handled correctly.

"It is time for my judgment. Take us to Emortono," God-Wrath ordered.

\*\*\*

A massive bloom appeared in the missing section of the Keeper fleet. The purple and pink chaotic field was larger than any ever seen by the CDF or in Dark Reign's fleet. It sparked, and various colors of lightning struck within it. Then the massive ship appeared: the flagship of God-Wrath. It was three times the size of the largest battleship ever built. It surged past its own fleet, on a direct course for the planet. A few ships stood in its way in a blockade. They fired their lasers, but to no effect. It rammed them, knocking them out of the way. This seemed to be the sign that everyone was waiting for. All ships moved closer to each other and engaged. No apparent strategy could be deciphered from the mix of conventional and laser weapons firing at each other. Fighters and bombers buzzed around the battle zone like flies. Bombers came in and launched large barrages of missiles and magnetic bombers at larger ships while fighters blew them up by the dozen.

CDF frigates put themselves in between the *Desolution* and the refugee camp, making it so that the massive ship could not get a direct shot with its electro-disk rail cannon. The disk powered up, spinning blue light within. Static lightning passed from one side of the disk to the other before a shot was fired on the refugee camp. It was blocked by a frigate, which exploded, and another frigate moved to its place. Defense platforms fired at the *Desolution*, wasting their time, as they were peashooters firing on a tank. The Keeper fleet followed the battleship, trying to catch up and surround the *Desolution* in a protective pattern. The fleet ships weren't as immune to the defense platforms and were taking heavy damage. They fired back, destroying the planetary defenses that had attacked them earlier. The fleet moved to protect the *Desolution* and create a barrier, guarding it against any stray ships that wanted to inflict damage.

***

"Dark Reign, we need to do something," demanded Chancellor Judy. "That flagship is popping my frigates like balloons."

Dark Reign paused the call to think for a moment. His hologram paced the bridge of the *Nightmare*. The Keeper fleet had ignored the main forces and gotten around them to the planet. He pondered how he would adjust his strategy. "Who is the admiral leading God-Wrath's forces?" he asked his communications officer.

"Skyfall, sir."

"That explains it. She loves to keep the fight as close to a planet as possible," Dark Reign muttered. "Resume the call."

The chancellor's image came back onscreen.

"Chancellor Judy, keep your forces following me. We are going after the fleet protecting that massive flagship, the *Desolution*, as it calls itself. It won't be able to get away or defend itself once we have superior numbers on it."

"I disagree. We need to cut off the head of this incursion. The other ships will return to their homeworlds without God-Wrath's leadership."

"There is no way we can muster that kind of firepower right now."

"What about the refugees? We can't leave the clones defenseless."

"We can, and we will. They're doomed, and we will be too if we don't stop discussing the plan and start implementing it." Dark Reign turned his head and nodded at the communications officer, ending the call. He ordered the main fleet to pursue the Keepers; they would leave the CDF behind if they had to.

The old, conventional fleet stayed behind and started to amass together. The older ships looked more damaged and broken than the newer fleet, and they hadn't engaged any ships yet. Turning off the hologram for a moment, Dark Reign looked around his physical location and gave a different set of orders. "Prepare the nukes. It's almost time," he barked.

The crew snapped to attention and executed his order with precision. They did not question why or when. They knew that whatever was going to happen, they would be a part of history today.

\*\*\*

Chancellor Judy surveyed the battle zone. "What's your assessment, Robert?" she asked as a laser shot back and forth across the room. She watched ships on both sides get hit too many times and explode, their pieces falling down to the planet below.

"Dark Reign is right. We can't focus enough of our forces on the *Desolution* until we get rid of the Keeper fleet," said Robert.

"Won't that help out the Acolytes a little too much? We have a different goal, and none of this military nonsense is going to change it," Chancellor Judy replied. "Order the defense force to break off and attack the *Desolution* at full force."

"But the Keeper fleet?" Robert asked.

"Let Dark Reign handle that."

\*\*\*

The CDF ships moved away from their assigned positions, exposing Dark Reign's fleet to the Keepers. The CDF ships flew closer to the *Desolution*, firing volleys of lasers. Their shots were connecting, but they were not having a large effect. You could tell from the *Desolution* that the shots that were getting through were having a slight effect. The Keepers started to defend it with rigor, their ships moving closer to it instead of taking action against Dark Reign's forces. They moved closer to the CDF ships and exchanged volleys at close range. Small fighters and bombers still swarmed around the *Desolution*. This distracted the CDF, as they had to contend with the fighters or be destroyed by them. They couldn't keep enough of their lasers firing at the *Desolution* to make a difference.

The *Desolution* sat in the middle of the battle like a quiet monument. It was still allowing the fleets to battle around it. The only action it took was to recharge the disk rails enough to fire a shot every ten minutes. The CDF still blocked it and the rest of the Keepers from getting direct shots at any of the targets that they had come for.

\*\*\*

"Order the main fleet back," ordered Dark Reign. "I want them to withdraw from the main fighting." A phase of transparency ran through his hologram.

"Sir, that will leave the CDF on their own against the Keeper fleet," said Officer Andre.

"Get everyone a safe distance away. It's too late for them," Dark Reign ordered. He was right. If the CDF fleet continued to engage the Keeper fleet, it risked being destroyed. The *Desolution* stood like a prize behind a glass cage, and they couldn't quite touch it without the attention of the Keeper attendants.

\*\*\*

Chancellor Judy ordered a full retreat. Two of the CDF ships tried to escape, propelling themselves out of the battle, only to be destroyed by the roaming squadrons of bombers that littered the battlefield. The ships needed cover fire or else they would be instantly destroyed. The CDF ships tried to count down the zero drives to make an escape. That was when the *Desolution* sprang to life. Its disk drive was no longer trying to destroy the camp of refugees. The light inside of it changed color and spun backward, creating an interdiction field. The *Desolution* was able to do the job of several smaller ships due to its massive size. The CDF was stuck. The only way they were going to get out of this was to fight their way out.

\*\*\*

"What is it doing?" asked the chancellor.

"It's an interdiction field, Chancellor," said General Robert. "We can't go to zero space. There is nothing we can do."

"Get everyone we have to fire on that ship," the chancellor ordered.

"We are already doing that."

# Galactic Mandate: A Radical Cause

"Then let's give it a more appetizing target. Have the frigates stop blocking their shot of the refugees and have them fly into the *Desolution*. Tell them that they sacrifice themselves for our way of life. This is the second Genetic War, as far as I am concerned."

She watched as the ships moved. They responded to her commands and moved forward, accelerating past battleships and battlecruisers until they threatened the *Desolution*. Their small size made it so they could quickly get around the other ships. She could see them speed up and try to ram into the *Desolution*, but the Keepers didn't allow it to happen. A coordinated burst of light hit the frigates, destroying them instantly.

"That's the opening we need. You are a genius, Chancellor," General Robert said. He called the other commanders over for a quick huddle. Not stopping to explain anything to the chancellor, he quickly gave orders to the other ships. They fired an impressive volley into the Keeper ships, launching any reserve fighters and bombers as well. This final onslaught caught the Keepers off-guard.

"The Keepers let their guard down by destroying the frigates," General Robert said as they watched Keeper ship after Keeper ship explode on their screen. The Keepers still outnumbered the CDF, but they were losing ships fast, and the renewed chaos kept them from organizing an effective counterattack.

"The day is almost won. Under my guidance, we will finally rid ourselves of this natural-born menace," Chancellor Judy said to applause. Everyone seemed to be releasing tension in an exaggerated, premature celebration. The room was ecstatic with cheer every time another Keeper ship exploded.

\*\*\*

"The CDF has turned the tide somehow," Officer Andre said.

"Then it is time. I am no longer needed here." The hologram of Dark Reign disappeared.

Officer Andre watched the battle unfold, unsure of his next command but opening up the normal channels so that they could receive orders when it was time for them to be involved once more.

*\*\*\**

Dark Reign walked off of his hologram platform and gave the order he had been waiting to give. "Tell every one of the old ships to fire every single nuke that they have."

The crew looked around, silent eyes moving from person to person, with each face asking the same question: *Did we just hear that?*

"You heard me. Fire the nukes. At the CDF and the Keepers."

*\*\*\**

The chancellor's battle room rang in alarm. She was confused as to what could cause an alarm in the middle of a battle. They were already getting fired at, and she'd seen fighters, bombers, and other ships trying their hardest to destroy the CDF and failing. That was when the wall-sized monitors in the room stopped blinking and started highlighting small dots that were increasing in size. They came from the old backup fleet that Dark Reign had thought he'd been hiding at the edge of the battle. She tried to see what they were, but there were thousands of them. She had a hard time trying to highlight just one. When she finally got the computers to zoom in on the small object, her eyes widened with the realization of just what she was looking at.

"Nukes!" she screamed, gathering the attention of the rest of the room.

General Robert turned, and his mouth dropped open as he whispered, "Fuck."

"Abandon ship!" the others screamed as they ran out of the room, leaving General Robert and Chancellor Judy to share a glance. They turned and ran with the rest of the crew.

# Galactic Mandate: A Radical Cause

***

Nuclear missiles hit Keeper and CDF ships without discretion. Some ships still had enough shielding to withstand one or even two missiles, but even the sturdier ships exploded from the number of missiles they were getting hit with. Entire fleets went up in balls of nuclear fire. Escape pods fired in all directions, and they blasted at full speed away from their host ships. They crashed into each other and into other ships, as there was a desperate rush to escape.

***

Ninety-six monitored his computer screen, looking for escape pods. He was aboard the *Saber*, a spare cruiser loaned to the sultan to run rescue missions during the battle. The sultan had been reluctant to accept the task, but with all that he owed Dark Reign, he was in no position to refuse. They didn't have any weapons, and due to its small size, white color, and medical markings, the ship avoided most of the fire from the battle. They picked up escape pods and brought them back to the medical station. Ninety-six enjoyed his new career. He had the position of updating the sultan, who was the captain of the ship, with the current battle situation. Farid was the first officer; he handled all the important calls that the sultan couldn't do himself.

"I can't wait until this battle is over," said the sultan. "We are to rule a whole new planet, Farid. That is what Dark Reign promised."

"I'm not sure if it's worth it," said Farid.

"Trust me. This is the best deal for us."

"You're in charge."

After listening in on the quick exchange, Ninety-six went back to monitoring his station. Surprised, he double-checked and then triple-checked his screen. The CDF was gone. A range of emotions flowed through him: excitement and a feeling of confused justice. They were technically on the same side, but Ninety-six hadn't forgotten that he'd just escaped their grasp. The screen filled with escape pods, and many were being destroyed as soon they registered. His thoughts on ethics and how he'd rather just ignore the CDF and leave them to their well-deserved fate had to wait. The ship needed to act fast, and he had a duty to fulfill. His fate had somehow gotten intertwined with that of the sultan and his crew of fighters, and he owed it to them to let them know about the escape pods.

They were already aware of the crazed action, though, because they could see it out the windows. A blind man could have seen the explosions and sudden graveyard of ships and floating bodies. "Sir, we are getting hundreds of distress signals from the CDF. They have escape pods everywhere. There are many appearing and disappearing. I don't know where you want to start."

"The tide of this battle is turning," the sultan replied, "and I don't want anything to do with it. Before you know it, everyone will be dead. Let's grab as many as we can, just the closest ones to us, and get out of here."

"What about the planet Dark Reign promised?" Farid asked.

"If it ends up like Emortono, we don't want it," the sultan explained.

Farid coordinated the rescue of the closest ships. They picked up everyone that they could before moving past the battle, getting distance between them and it. They watched as the *Desolution* dropped its interdiction field and reversed its disk rails. It shot its rail cannon and blew up several of Dark Reign's ships in the main fleet. The escape pods were flagged on Ninety-six's computers. He turned towards the sultan, who just shook his head. They were filling up quickly, and there was nothing they could do for the others. It felt odd that they were going out of their way for the CDF and not Dark Reign's forces. Ninety-six wanted to say something, to complain or object, but being the newest member of the sultan's group, he just didn't have the authority to do it.

# Galactic Mandate: A Radical Cause

"Pull up the cargo monitor as soon as the last escape pod is loaded and countdown the zero drive. We are getting out of here," the sultan ordered.

"Yes, sir," Farid replied.

They watched as random clones left the escape pods. They picked up everyone, and there were specific bays for each group. They picked up a few Keepers and put them in detention. They also picked up a few of Dark Reign's men if their escape pods were close enough, but the majority were clones. Then Ninety-six gasped. His mouth dropped open in awe.

"Oh fuck," the sultan muttered.

"Shit! Start the countdown. Now!" Farid yelled.

The countdown started with the ship's computer giving everyone a warning. Then it counted down in a computerized female voice. The sultan and Ninety-six ignored the countdown; their eyes were fixed on the security monitor.

"That's the chancellor," Ninety-six finally squeaked out.

"It sure fucking is," said the sultan.

Ninety-six watched as she disembarked from her escape pod with Ninety-seven. His eyes grew even bigger when he saw that Ninety-seven was pregnant.

# Chapter 50

The sea had reached their necks, and the oxygen devices had reached their maximum lifespan. Kai and Danica kicked their feet as they swam. Kai looked rough; a patchy beard had grown in the time they had been in prison. Danica's hair had also become unruly, and so had CJ's.

"I think this is it, Kai. we can't hold out any longer," said Danica.

"Good riddance. You Acolytes just make everything worse," CJ replied.

The fog was thick that day. They could barely see each other. They could barely see beyond their cages.

Laser fire seared through the grounded clouds, creating a light show as the bass from explosions assaulted their ears. The glowing lights of a descending ship haloed above them. The loud booms of conventional weapons exploding against the rocks coincided with lasers piercing the sky. CJ, Danica, and Kai looked up in amazement as the prison fell quickly to the foreign ship. Guards exploded when grenades met their bodies. Ships were called in to respond but were blown out of the sky. They created puffs of fireballs in the slightly yellow but mostly white fog.

There was a startlingly loud clank as two men landed on top of the cage. They were attached to a rope. "Stand back," the buff man said as he used a giant saw on the bars, sending sparks everywhere. The name on the uniform said: "Jay." He appeared to be enjoying himself as he cut a circle large enough for a person to fit through.

"Time to go," said the man with a uniform showing the name "Baruti."

Kai reached up and grabbed his hand. He was pulled up and attached to a rope that took him up into the ship. Next was Danica. She reached up and was met by Jay's strong hands. He gave her a wink as he attached her to the rope. CJ reached up to follow. Baruti slapped away her hand. "She's not on the list."

This was met by a forceful punch from Jay. "I don't give a fuck about the list. She is hot. My mom said to never pass up a woman in need."

Baruti stumbled back. CJ watched with seeking eyes, but she didn't show any emotion. She wasn't her usual confident self. Jay reached down and extended a hand towards her. CJ looked at both of them and then gave Baruti a slight grin. The world seemed to be quiet as she stood still, just keeping her head above water. "Come on. I'm not going to keep my hand out all day," said Jay.

"I told you. The list is there for a reason. We don't have time for this," said Baruti.

CJ grabbed Jay's hand, and they were off.

On the ship, Michael inspected his rescues. "You have been in prison for a while, and there is a lot to catch you up on. I'm going to let Dark Reign and the fancy pants do that."

"Where is Mantis?" Kai asked.

"His extraction is getting too political and is no longer a priority," Michael replied. "Ever since the wedding, we can't tell if he's even considered a hostage anymore. I don't think he's going to last more than a cycle myself."

Kurt steered their cloaked ship out of the atmosphere as everyone talked in the cargo hold. Death's Witness went back to mostly checking their weapons while their leader filled in the hostages. The room smelled clean, almost sterile. The only aroma a person could detect was that of the oils used to clean the guns every once in a while. It was quiet except for a classical arrangement playing to calm down the ex-hostages while they prepared for zero space.

"What is CJ doing here?" Kai asked, and she smiled.

"Who?" asked Michael.

"I think he means this one. She's my new girlfriend," Jay said. CJ responded with a confident smile.

Jax stared at the couple. He didn't want to feel left out. "I think she likes me better," he interjected.

"I'm more than either you can handle. Although you both are my type of man." She winked her left eye at Jay and her right eye at Jax. They both had wide, toothy smiles as they backed away to the walls of the ship, watching over their new guest with fantasies of the future. Kai didn't bother with a response. He knew from this group's reputation that there was not much he could do.

"What would Boulder say?" Danica quipped.

Her remark was met with a quick sneer from CJ. "I don't know who this twig thinks she is talking about, but no man can match my Boulder."

Jay held up his arms, flexing and showing each one off. "Skinny girl is just jealous of us, bro," said Jax.

"Cut the chatter. We're almost to the *Nightmare*," Michael said.

The cloaked ship arrived out of zero space in the middle of the battle. God-Wrath's Keeper forces were engaging Dark Reign's military, and the scene was chaos. The crew buckled themselves down as the artificial gravity shifted with the turns of the ship.

"I've had it. We don't kill Acolytes," said Michael. "We don't harm our own. I told Dark Reign this wasn't going to end up well. Set a new course, Kurt. We are going to get out of here."

The ship was struck by stray fire, dropping the cloak and exposing it. "This is very bad," Kurt said. Taking advantage of the situation, he quickly switched the music from classical to a rough urban style.

"Is that really important right now?" Kai asked.

"It helps me focus," Kurt replied. He saw that they had started to flag every ship on the battlefield from green to red. "We're in an unmarked ship in the middle of a civil war. We are an active target for everyone." Kurt started maneuvering, trying to get some distance from the battle. They dodged shots of opportunity as they watched from the windows and on monitors as missiles, lasers, and even some low-yield nukes flew past. Missed by laser fire, two missiles locked onto the ship's signature. They appeared to have been fired by Dark Reign's forces.

"Look. We're about to be shot down by her own side," Kurt vented.

"What?" Danica asked.

"Nothing, sweetheart. We'll be out of here in no time."

The missiles zigged and zagged, closely matching their course as they twisted and turned through space, swirling around each other as they closed in. "Get these things off of us, Kurt," Michael ordered. He unbuckled himself and stood over Kurt, micromanaging his console and pushing buttons for countermeasures.

Kai started to pray while Danica looked intently at the piloting crew. CJ grabbed Jay's hand on her left while squeezing Jax's on her right. "Midnight, get on the turret," Michael ordered.

Midnight unbuckled and rushed to the turret station. He popped open a joystick and started to spray bullets at the oncoming missiles. Kurt continued to weave throughout the battle. "The zero drive is almost ready. Only a couple of seconds longer. Buckle up. It might be jumpy."

"I've survived much thicker situations than this cushy space battle," Michael replied.

Extra fired another line of conventional bullets at the missiles, closely watching his tracer fire until he hit one. An explosion occurred, and the threat was gone. The two missiles disappeared from the screen for a second, and then one reappeared. Michael was already relaxed from seeing them disappear, and he didn't have time to react when the remaining missile tumbled vertically into the ship. It exploded, sending him headfirst into the bulkhead.

Danica popped out of her seat and rushed over to see to the welfare of her rescuers. She looked into his eyes just as his soul seemed to leave the body behind, and then the damaged ship entered zero space. "Major, Major, respond!" she yelled.

"It's no use," Baruti said behind her. He placed a comforting hand on her shoulder. "He's gone." Danica's eyes started to water as she was flooded with emotions.

Kai asked, "Where are we going?"

"That's a good question," said Baruti. "Kurt?"

"I don't know where we should go. I just plotted a course away from here. There is nothing but empty space waiting for us."

Extra came back from the turret, and his eyes locked on the dead major. "Maybe that's a good thing. I'm done dodging missiles for a warrantless war," he said.

"Our major is dead for ten seconds, and you are already talking treason!" Jay yelled, getting in Extra's face. Their eyes deadlocked, and their fists were balled. Baruti got in between them, pushing both back a couple of inches. A combination of musty smells intertwined in the air.

"Going back is not an option. Not until we see how this crap pans out," said Baruti.

"I have a suggestion," said Kai. "Please be aware that being the highest-ranking officer on the ship, I ordered Death's Witness to follow me and hunt down Dr. Tom. He started all this crap. His technology needs to be dealt with."

The muscular men looked back, confused and contemplative.

"We all know that's unsanctioned," said Danica.

"I know some space pirates we can join," said CJ. "We can make our own fate, boys. There's plenty of profit to be made in the times ahead."

"I don't believe I'm saying this, but I don't disagree," Danica said.

Jax stepped up and removed his hand from CJ's embrace. "I'd rather keep my oath and duty than become a low-life pirate."

Kurt turned to look at the others. "Do we not have any respect for the dead? We just lost a major."

"We need to decide this now," said Baruti, "before we are adrift in space. It's rough, but we are Death's Witness for a reason. We can't just stop because we lost one of our own."

Extra spoke up again. "I'm down for pirating. I could use some extra cash. We don't have to make a career of it. It could be a vacation."

"We're definitely not taking a vacation," said Jax.

"I could use a legendary super black ops team," said Kai. "There is no way I'll be able to capture Dr. Tom without you. I've already tried once and failed."

"Miserably," Danica added.

"We don't fail," Extra and Jay said in unison, causing them both to feel their own skin.

Baruti turned to Extra and saluted. "Extra is the highest-ranking Death's Witness. He should be the one to decide."

"No," said Kai. "I am the highest-ranking officer. You will do what I say."

"No offense, but no one cares," said Kurt. "It's Midnight's call."

Jay and Jax's eyes met. They gave each other a head nod, and then Jay spoke up. "You already know where I stand."

"It'll be worth your time. Just one job," CJ begged.

"So, where are we going?" Danica asked.

Extra rubbed his chin and lifted his eyebrows. "This will be exciting, if I do say so myself. I don't know what our fate will be, but I do know we need to get out of this war. Set a course for Freedom Station. I think I have a few ideas." He smiled, and the white chalk flaked off his black skin.

# Chapter 51

The head Keeper clutched at his heart, sobbing as he watched so many of his brethren die in the nuclear fire that Dark Reign had unleashed. God-Wrath and Skyfall were close behind. Skyfall threw her command console as far as she could, destroying it against the wall. The bridge crew interrupted the grim scene to inform God-Wrath that they were being hailed by the *Nightmare*. Dark Reign appeared as a hologram on the bridge with them.

"I have destroyed the CDF. I took that kill from you. For all the talking and the plotting, I did something you've been scheming to do for years, and it only took me a couple of seconds. You are a failure. Surrender now. The time of living gods is over. You have no purpose anymore, no calling, and no fleet. Do the only responsible thing and surrender." His hologram disappeared. The fighting ceased as Dark Reign's fleet waited for a response.

"He's right," Skyfall said.

"Don't listen to her!" the head Keeper yelled, recomposing himself. "We need to fall back to Keeper space and regroup."

"I am only here for the cause," replied Skyfall, "and Dark Reign completed the cause. I can't believe this, but I agree with the head Keeper. We need to regroup and invade CDF space. There will be no one to defend it now."

"Never. I'm not running, and I'm not surrendering. The fight isn't over," God-Wrath announced.

"We are the only ones left," Skyfall announced.

"And this ship is more than capable isn't it?" God-Wrath asked.

"Yes, it is. But we should go back to the forge and make more," the head Keeper whispered in response.

"Skyfall, don't tell me you are out of strategies," said God-Wrath.

"I'm not," she replied.

"Then get it together. It's time to finally show them what the embodiment of my wrath can do," God-Wrath ordered.

Skyfall got on the intercom and commanded, "Every fighter in reserve, get out there now. Bring the pain."

"That is more like it. But it won't be enough. Don't we have some of those new laser cannons on this ship? Activate them."

"We do, but if we bring the cannons online at the same time as the disk rail, it will drop the shields. We will be exposed," Skyfall warned.

"Do it. And blow up that refugee camp," God-Wrath commanded.

She quickly moved to another command console, pushing the officer who was standing there out of her way. She punched in the codes, entering in passwords and commands. Then she stopped before entering the last one. "Are you sure? Your mother is at that camp," she asked.

"Yes," God-Wrath replied.

The shields dropped, and the disk rails fired on the planet. Large laser cannons rose from the depths of the ships, four on top and two on the bottom. They wiggled free from enclosures and could each fire in a ninety-degree arc, which was needed because they were already taking heavy damage. Dark Reign's fleet had started firing again as soon as they'd seen the disk rails charging. Ship after ship was destroyed by the *Desolution*'s new laser cannons, the state-of-the-art offensive weaponry surprising Dark Reign's forces and quickly overwhelming them.

The *Desolution* was paying a price for its offensive barrage. It had clear, visible holes throughout its hull. The reserve fighters and bombers didn't last long even though there was a fair amount of them. Explosions occurred throughout the ship, but somehow, it kept itself together.

Finally, the conventional weapons of Dark Reign's fleet finally made it through the *Desolution*'s countermeasures, destroying most of the ship. Only two of its laser cannons remained. The main fleet of Dark Reign was all but destroyed. Even the *Nightmare* had been destroyed by the end of the exchange.

"That's it, right? We've killed Dark Reign. There is no one left to oppose you. We win," said the head Keeper.

Dark Reign's hologram appeared again. "I'm not so easy to kill."

"He must be on a ship in the old fleet," Skyfall suggested.

"No use in hiding it anymore. I am," he replied. "Give it up, God-Wrath. Your last salvo was surprising, but it wasn't enough."

"Like I said before. Never," said God-Wrath.

"Have it your way." Dark Reign ended the holographic call.

\*\*\*

The old, conventional fleet shot off the last two of the *Desolution*'s cannons. The disk rails charged up but no longer fired. The immense ship was disabled. That didn't stop the threat, as it pointed its front at what was left of the old fleet. Just a few ships resisted God-Wrath's control of the empire. The *Desolution* started its engine, chasing the old fleet as they fired at it.

A single ship emerged from zero space. It raced towards the battle, hailing what remained of the two fleets. A holographic message was broadcasted. "This is Tyron Jamal. I've come to negotiate a truce. Cease this aggression at once. Do what is best for the empire. My ship is small, and it's not the best, but it's in much better shape than what I see here. Whoever does not cease this senseless act of aggression will be destroyed, and I will negotiate with whoever is left."

\*\*\*

Dark Reign yelled, "Never!"

# Galactic Mandate: A Radical Cause

The bridge crew stopped. The captain of the ship, a young officer, shook his head. "No, no, no... I don't want to die. I'm not ready." The crew turned and looked at Dark Reign.

"You will do your duty, Captain," he said.

"Not if it's a personal vendetta. Isn't that why we are rebelling? So we can live under the rule of law?" the captain replied.

A long silence followed. Dark Reign read the room, and he thought of his daughters. The pain hit him like a ton of bricks.

"God-Wrath, he's a monster. He only cares about one thing. I took that away from him. But I cared about more than that. I cared about my family. God-Wrath has done his best to take that away from me. But I forgot about my other family. My brothers in arms. I can't let him do that to me. I can't let him change me. Thank you. You reminded me of what I once was. Not just you, Captain, but all of you. I wouldn't ask if it wasn't important..." Dark Reign looked around at what amounted to children. They were as young as his daughter Dark Cleo. They looked at him like she did. That's when he stopped.

"All right..." He paused and waited for his brothers, his children, to release the tension in their faces. "Get me a channel. Let's negotiate."

\*\*\*

"Enough is enough. I'm sending the signal to stand down!" Skyfall yelled as she sent the signal to decelerate the ship. The crew felt the shift in force as the main engines cut out.

"Turn them back on!" God-Wrath commanded from his chair. His hands dropped, and he forcefully strode down the steps.

"Arrest him," Skyfall commanded. The crew didn't respond, but only put their guns down in submission.

God-Wrath drew his sword and charged at Skyfall. She dodged, smacking him in the back of the head. He swung wildly, slicing her clothes. She moved to grab a gun. Pointing it at God-Wrath's head, she hesitated. His eyes locked with hers. The edges of her eyes dropped down. She slightly cocked her head to the side and then back. This gave God-Wrath the opening he needed. He swung the sword across her chest, slicing her deeply. The blood spilled down her clothes and dripped to the floor. The rage left God-Wrath's face, the anger dripping away like Skyfall's blood. He dropped his sword and grabbed her. Tears instantly filled his eyes.

"Don't die for nothing... like me," Skyfall commanded as consciousness left her.

God-Wrath yelled in agony and wept. He screamed so wildly his voice left him as he took in air. Skyfall hung lifelessly in his arms. "What have I done? What have I done?"

"You have gained peace. I see you have slain the person responsible for all this hardship," the head Keeper announced to holograms of Dark Reign and Tyron. They nodded in agreement. God-Wrath turned and looked at them with tears in his eyes, his teeth clenched.

The head Keeper moved in and whispered, "We will avenge this another day."

# *Epilogue*

Five years later

Ninety-six flew into Emortono, accompanied by his band of misfits and the elite guards formerly commanded by the sultan. The crew of the small frigate was a band of about ten people.

"All right, crew," he said, "listen up. I don't want any problems for the next thirty minutes. We are arriving at Emortono's DMZ." The planet was now encircled by a gigantic ring of destroyed ships and the defense platforms of the empires that shared it.

"We have to deliver these age accelerators to the Southern Palace," Ninety-six continued.

"Do we have passcodes for the blockade?" asked Farid.

"Only for the southern hemisphere. If we fly at the wrong angle and cross the equator, God-Wrath's forces will fire on us."

"Those zealots have only gotten worse since the armistice."

"Yeah, they have."

"We drop in to deliver the goods and hope nobody is trying to double-cross us, right, boss?"

"Damn right."

They landed at the ruined palace, which was being retrofitted as a cathedral.

"Everything is going fine so far," said Farid.

"Yeah, a little too smoothly if you ask me," replied Ninety-six.

Upon arriving, Dark Reign's assistant came to greet them. "Load the cargo in the back and down the hall," she said. "I don't trust my men to be discreet enough. There are spies everywhere on this planet, you know."

"Yeah, we do, 'cause half of them are yours," Ninety-six replied.

"That's beside the point."

The band on her wrist started blinking wildly, alerts for what seemed to be urgent messages. Ninety-six and his crew were still handling crates as they became quiet, listening in on the communication from one of the military leaders of the planet.

"What do you mean both fleets are retreating?" the assistant said. "Is the planet undefended? Impossible."

Earsplitting screams came from the sky as dropships and large spaceships descended.

"They are back!" shouted Farid.

Then they heard it: a pulsating pitch that brought everyone in the vicinity to their knees. It was the last thing Ninety-six would ever hear.

# *Epilogue 2*

Scarlet Lilly turned off the monitors. She listened as advisors and diplomats chattered, suggesting a wide range of political moves and options. She listened as they yammered and haggled.

She looked outside at her flower garden, one of the vastest in the galaxy. It amazed the senses with its wonderful rows of colors that led off into infinity. She carefully slipped out of the room, unnoticed by the magistrates and diplomats. They continued to bicker without her presence.

Walking slowly across the field, she reached one of the many gazebos. Servants scattered about in their white clothes covered with different floral designs. They rushed away as she approached, leaving alone a woman who clashed drastically with the surroundings.

"Sister, have you heard about the disrespect that has fallen on our family?" Scarlet asked.

"I have," her sister replied.

"Have you come to do something about it? I know I used to find your skills to be so unsuitable for a woman of your stature, but they might actually come in handy now."

"I can help you, but I need you to let me back in."

"Are you sure? What I need is difficult. To get our family back in its proper place is going to take some hard work."

"What you need is for me to get the Tri-cess out of your way, and I'm the only one who can do it."

"Kill the Tri-cess, and I'll see that your excommunication is removed and you are no longer hunted as a war criminal, Snapdragon."

"But I said let me in."

"I can give you a fresh start," said Scarlet, "but we all know that politics and fancy dresses aren't for you."

"A fresh start, and all it will cost is one dead queen and two dead concubines," replied Snapdragon.

# Galactic Mandate: A Radical Cause

## Galactic Mandate: A Radical Cause

If you like this book, please leave a review. The only way I can decide whether to commit more time to these characters and this series is by getting feedback from you, the readers. Your opinion matters to me. I have only so much time to craft new stories. Help me invest that time wisely. Plus, reviews are the only way an author can level up and defeat space pirates.

## M.R. Richardson

## About me

I have roots in California and Washington state. My love for science fiction goes all the way back to the 1990s. I've always wanted to explore new ideas and imagine new concepts. I strive for innovation always and I am glad you decided to take this journey with me. Keep an eye out for me because I love to go to science fiction & fantasy conventions. If you see me there please say hello so we can talk.

www.MR-Richardson.com